When to Go into the Water

When to Go into the Water

a novel
Lawrence Sutin

Sarabande Books
LOUISVILLE, KENTUCKY

Managing Editor
Sarabande Books, Inc.
2234 Dundee Road, Suite 200
Louisville, KY 40205

Library of Congress Cataloging-in-Publication Data

Sutin, Lawrence, 1951-
    When to go into the water : a novel / by Lawrence Sutin. — 1st ed.
        p.   cm.
    Includes bibliographical references and index.
    ISBN 978-1-932511-72-7 (pbk. : alk. paper)
    1. Experimental fiction. I. Title.
    PS3619.U8838W47 2009
    813'.6—dc22   2008028296

ISBN-13: 978-1-932511-72-7

Cover image: "Headless Swan, Wetless Water" © Copyright 2009 by Brennan Vance. Provided courtesy of the artist.

Cover and text design by Charles Casey Martin

Manufactured in Canada
This book is printed on acid-free paper.

Sarabande Books is a nonprofit literary organization.

The Kentucky Arts Council, a state agency in the Commerce Cabinet, provides operational support funding for Sarabande Books with state tax dollars and federal funding from the National Endowment for the Arts, which believes that a great nation deserves great art.

This project is supported in part by an award from the National Endowment for the Arts.

To Sarah, with love and gratitude for the idea

HECTOR DE SAINT-AUREOLE, the elusive—or shall we say simply unremembered?—author of *When to Go into the Water*, was born in 1900, the sole child of peasant farmers in the east of France. His mother and father were quiet persons who, like sunflowers, flourished in their daylong labors and drooped when indoors. Hector remembered how his mother recurrently hummed a tune that she could make sound happy or sad but to which she never sang the words. His father would sit by the hearth after supper and carve tiny fearsome top-combed roosters from kindling. Both parents believed in the value of reading the Bible, of living by it by their own lights, and of staying clear of churches, which they regarded as dens of temptation in which those who paid heed only to appearances gave over the care of their souls to frocked collars. Hector was breastfed and thereafter seldom touched by either of them. His mother schooled him in letters and arithmetic and Hector read the two books to be found in the cottage, a Bible and a volume of selections from the lives of the saints with prints interspersed here and there showing dying men pierced by arrows to their hearts and dying women looking to heaven as flames licked their bodies. Hector liked the saints best in the early paragraphs of their lives when they were still being tempted. But all of them gave in to purity so easily. Even as a little boy, Hector came to prefer the succubi who breathed upon his neck and cheeks and whispered into his ear at night and by and large understood him as he wished himself to be understood.

WHEN HECTOR WAS FOURTEEN, World War One came to their farm. The German troops requisitioned, shot, and ate the goats, sheep, and chickens but spared the four dairy cows that produced butter and milk, nearly all of which went to the invaders as well. But the family was not harmed. Once a German soldier sat Hector by his side on a bench outside a neighboring farmhouse and, as two French milkmaids looked on, shared a bowl of soup with the boy. A fellow soldier took a photograph that later appeared in a Munich newspaper to refute British propaganda that called the Kaiser's forces "Barbarians." The photograph worked because of Hector's frailty—he was smaller than his years and less use on the farm than his father would have liked—all the more highlighted by his being outfitted in a gingham smock his mother had years before sewn overlarge to make it last. No question the boy's brown eyes so yearned for the *Mittagssuppe* in the soldier's spoon. Neither his parents nor Hector ever knew of this publicity triumph, the moment when Hector exercised the greatest influence over the world that he ever would. But Hector thereafter became a favorite among the German soldiers whose camp occupied what had been the family's pasturage. They invited him over to their nighttime fires and gave him cigarettes and schnapps and let him listen to their stories in mixed German and French—the latter for the boy's sake—about women who were insistent about their virtue until a man slapped them, and then they behaved and showed themselves to be as coarse as the most depraved soldier on leave from the front lines. To Hector, this had the stink of lies told by liars who took what they wanted from war or women. He did not dare to call them what they were, nor to say that love was passionately gentle—his body and the Bible agreed on that much. One night one of the soldiers wondered aloud if perhaps their coy little Hector required a slap as well. Laughter then bellowed from all the soldiers and Hector braced himself for a blow to his face. Instead they pinched his cheeks and his behind and when he blushed and begged them to stop they pinched and laughed all the more. He ran away back to the cottage which he and his parents were permitted to retain because of its cramped squalor and proximity to the dairy barn. Hector never went back to the troop fires though he missed the cigarettes. He yearned for the war to slaughter the soldiers on both sides, as he already knew in his heart that all armies talked about love that way.

Hector eager for a taste of soup, October 1914.

ONE OF THE READERS of *When to Go into the Water* was an old Nova Scotian who emigrated in the 1980s to Jamaica where he lived in a three-storied white house with a grand portico atop a green hillside along the north coast. His daughter had married the Jamaican owner of a fashionable restaurant in Port Antonio that featured a cocktail named after Noel Coward, the master of the drawing-room farce, who had retired to Jamaica and frequented the place in his last years. Coward once brought his houseguest Winston Churchill to the restaurant. A photograph of the three of them—the English playwright, the English prime minister, the Jamaican restauranteur—now greeted customers as they entered. All this was enough to assure the postcolonial fortune of the Nova Scotian's son-in-law, who indulged his wife's desire to have her poor elderly father come to live out his days in their house, with Jamaican servants to tend to him until he passed. For over sixty years—from his early teens until his departure for Jamaica at his daughter's insistence—the Nova Scotian had earned his living as a gatherer of herbs, typically in the evening hours: herbs for digestion, excretion, and sleep, herbs for the healing of injured livestock and the easing of human toothache. Removed from his Nova Scotian forests and faced with the rife palms and bushes of Jamaica, he felt himself a man from whom sight and sense had been taken. His daughter considered returning him to Canada, but her husband—unwilling to allow that he could not arrange for an old man's happiness—suggested distracting him instead. There were ornately bound books that decorated the mantel of the marble-faced hearth of his restaurant. Have him read some of those, or have the servants read to him. So it was that one night, as an old and drunk Nova Scotian tried to find sleep, the weary voice

11

of an old and sober Jamaican woman, who would have preferred that the Nova Scotian listen to the BBC, recited to him the few lines in *When to Go into the Water* that Hector devoted to his native land: "Why should the landscape of my childhood matter more than the passing view from my taxicab in a strange city? I have never wanted to sink my soul into any setting—let them float near and then far away. The craving for the familiar leads to enslavement. From the time of my youth I sought to cast myself adrift. Pity those who cannot endure the swirling of life." The Nova Scotian, hearing these words, bristled and pitied Hector in turn as a man who had never knelt in joy in the moonlight upon having found, at last, in a wooded grove he had worked for decades, mandragora.

THE OCCUPATION OF THE FARM was especially hard for Hector's father who disliked strangers of all kinds even in peacetime. As the war drew to a close and the German forces were in retreat, the father realized that his farm would be restored to him and that, with the debt he would run up for new livestock, it would be better to have only two mouths to feed. His faith revealed to him that a sacrament of departure was necessary. Hector would later remember icy water poured from a stout oaken bucket down his brow, his eyelids, his nostrils. His father was speaking to him in a voice that ran down him as well. Why, his father asked, do men speak of faith as if it were as common as salt when it is as dear as saffron? Faith is the water sprung from the rock in the desert by Moses. Faith is what I bid you to have as you leave us, my son. I baptize you in the waters of the righteous. Amen, and as Jesus was the most beloved of sons, so you Hector are to me. Hector, who was by now chilled through by the slow steady pouring from the oaken bucket, began to shiver and to sob with relief that his days with this man, who lied about love just as the soldiers did, were over.

THE MEMORY OF THE BAPTISM could have proved a lifelong anguish for Hector. Fortunately, in accord with the most loving of his teachings, Jesus made a conciliatory appearance two days later as Hector sat alone beside a creek, readying himself to depart from the only home he had ever known. Hector hadn't prayed for a vision of Jesus as so many do. He would have much preferred a sight of Jeanne d'Arc mounted in her rags and armor, or of St. Brigitte with her spilling tresses aglow in the service of the Lord. One explanation for the favor shown Hector is that Jesus appears to those who reject the teachings of which Jesus himself is weary, having witnessed their fate. Such rejecters neither seek nor expect the Jesus of the Bible, whom they presume dead. And so, with them, Jesus is able to dress as he wishes and to speak the local patois, as he did with Hector. The guise of Jesus was that of a locksmith, one who is capable of springing open stubborn doors. This locksmith now paused from his trekking from village to village to take a rest beside the creek. He asked if Hector's parents had locks in need of repair and Hector replied that his parents had no need of locks as they had nothing. And you, the locksmith asked, is there anything of which you are in need? Hector disliked talk for its own sake. Nor did he wish to wheedle coins from this stranger by telling him of the poverty that would face him in his travels. So Hector remained silent and squinted out into the stream and fell into a reverie in which he saw a great pike with a golden crown ascend from the ripples and spit fountain-like a stream of water into the hand of the locksmith, who was now surrounded with an aureole of light. The locksmith poured the water from his palm onto Hector's head. A voice spoke into Hector's ear: "May you always forego the persuasions of others, no matter how seemingly

14

certain. Follow your own uncertainties instead. Then come to heaven and tell me what you have seen and felt and done, for there are times when I am lonely there and long for tales of life." And it was so, for the voice Hector now heard was that of a succubus.

BY THE LOWEST-CLASS PASSAGE he made his way to Paris and found work as a renderer in an abattoir. There were, in the pitiful boarding house in which he had his own cot but not his own room, no facilities for bathing, and the public houses were beyond his means. Day and night, Hector smelled like blood and death to himself. When he walked the sidewalks of Paris people veered into traffic to avoid him. It was in this period that Hector first fell in love—from afar. She was a peddler with red hair, a pale freckled face, faint blue eyes and upturned lips that seemed, to Hector, saintly. Fruits were her wares, apples and lemons and pears and now and then cherries and grapes. She never so much as glanced at her customers until they expressly hailed her, ready to pay. And then it was their coins, not their faces, that she studied. She was ten years older than Hector which Hector didn't realize though it wouldn't have mattered to him. He went out of his way to walk past her stall in the marketplace. He bought fruit when his yearning to speak to her became unbearable, but while buying the fruit he couldn't find words and she noticed only a pervasive blood stench. He did manage to observe that she wasn't wearing a wedding ring. The conviction grew within Hector that seizing her attention was the sole task of his life. He knew he was not unhandsome. There were women who looked upon him and smiled at what they saw. Hector was not one to smile back or to speak, for he wanted nothing from them. But from Francoise he wanted everything, though the means of telling her this was not yet within him. Hector was driven to a stratagem that unnerved him from the moment he pursued it.

ONE OF THE READERS of *When to Go into the Water* found it in an old bookstore in Cleveland in the late 1970s. The guy who ran the store made his money on the men's magazines and hard-boiled erotic pulps in the front, but there were waist-high swinging doors leading to the back where you had to turn on the lights yourself if you wanted to browse. The shelves were old wooden fruit and vegetable crates that still emanated the smell of rotted produce that danced alongside the smells of beer and vomit coming from a toilet in the far corner. Up front, the owner was smoking a Chesterfield, ashing in an ashtray shaped like a mermaid with upturned breast stacks like an ocean liner, and eyeballing our man, the browser who had ignored the porn to see what sorts of old books were back there. The browser had come in after noticing a sign in the window: "Liquidation of private library." Whose? the browser had asked. Private, the owner had told him. That and you'll find the prices in pencil on the flyleaves and back through those swinging doors. And in a Boy Blue Pears crate the browser came upon a copy of *When to Go into the Water*, which he took to be an arcane text on naval strategy and purchased for $2.00. He stopped on the way home for a package of Chesterfields and that night, ashing in an ashtray shaped like a snake curled in on itself, he read Hector's book, drew a warm bath, got in, kept reading and smoking past midnight, stepped at last out of the water grown cold, his naked skin fitting him oblong and bumpy and tight like a freshly picked pear.

THE NAME OF THE RED-HAIRED PEDDLER was Francoise. She had no wedding ring as she had torn it from her finger five years earlier, the day her husband disappeared and left to her the care of three children. These days, while Francoise worked her fruit stall, her mother kept watch at home on the boy, Gabriel, now eight, who was a devil; the girl, Gabrielle, now seven, who was a devil as well; and the girl, Marguerite, now six, who was a servitor of devils. As for Francoise herself, she was as finished with men as a drowning man reaching shore would be finished with swimming. It astonished her that still they sniffed and smiled at her as if, with her children squabbling by her side in the evenings, she should require in addition their sagging bellies and poking lust. It made Francoise's mother laugh as well, when the two of them sat by the fire and spoke of what now seemed the good fortune of losing their husbands. For the elder woman, the loss had come when the drunkard father of Francoise was attacked by two knife-wielding thieves while returning home from a tavern late and soused. After having surrendered his purse and been told to go on his way, the father attempted to tackle them both as they turned their backs to him. Instead he missed and landed headfirst on the flagstones, knocking himself unconscious. The two thieves wished no part of the unnecessary crime of murder, but as they were annoyed by his lunge at them they laid him face first into a drain ditch in which, that night, in a heavy rain that kept one of the thieves awake as it scratched on the roof of his hovel like Satan's talons come to claim their prey, he drowned.

IN A BACK STREET OF MONTMARTRE there resided a magus who, it was said, had studied under the grand occultist Eliphas Levi and was endowed with the power of fashioning binding love potions. To the door of this magus Hector came one evening—a door at the top of a winding garret stairway the walls of which were begrimed with what seemed to Hector to be the smears left by bloody hands that had sought vainly to claw their way out of their fate. The worn brass knocker in the shape of a smiling gargoyle produced, upon Hector's release of it, a thud rather than a clang, a thud that made Hector think of the many who had come before him with desires that seemed, to each of them, to hold the key to their life's joy—a joy that the gargoyle could no longer, after so many years of service, bring itself to sound with any fervor. The door opened and the magus, who went by the sole name of Stanislaus, waved Hector into his chamber. Stanislaus was bald, but the surviving black hair of his temples and neck flowed over his shoulders while his black moustaches settled over his lips like an octopus at rest. He wore a black velvet robe, a shirt of red silk, black velveteen pantaloons, and tooled Persian slippers with upturned toes. Around his neck was a chain of rose gold from which hung a pantacle of jadeite. The chamber in which they sat was lined with shelves brimming with leather-spined tomes with infernal Latin titles in gold Gothic lettering. It took little more than a minute of whispered intimations by the magus to convince Hector that the week's wages it had taken the young man three months to save was not too great a price to pay for a tiny pouch of powder, the ingredients in which included (only this much would Stanislaus say) the pulverized tongue of a salamander and the particulate from the tears of an undine magically summoned by Stanislaus from her grotto in the

19

depths of the sea where she would have preferred to remain with her Triton lover. As Stanislaus explained to the rapt Hector, one surreptitiously poured the powder into one's palm and then let it fall all but invisibly into the hair of the desired one while silently reciting a secret spell composed by the magus himself. After having made Hector repeat the spell three times with care — for Stanislaus, wary of the authorities, would write nothing down — he bade Hector depart with haste and happy anticipation. The bloody hand smears seemed, on Hector's descent, mere remnants of worn paint. A furtive seeker on her way up to the magus passed him, concealing her face with a magenta scarf.

THE WORLD IS FILLED WITH MANY THINGS, most of all with secrets. We all carry secrets in our pockets, because we are all fearful, lying, or mad. Such were the musings of Hector as he returned to his boarding house with his tiny pouch of magical powder in his pocket. A rain began to fall and Hector wrapped his right hand around the pouch so that the powder inside would not moisten and prematurely expire. For Stanislaus had explained that it would be the subtle moistures of the beloved one's hair and scalp that would trigger the powder's subcutaneous entry into the blood and thence into the left rear of the brain where lay the centers of amativeness and reproductive love. The rain turned to mist and fog and Hector made his way through the dimly lit gaslight streets with difficulty, at one point stepping knee-depth into a gutter in which swirled horse manure, the stem-ends of cabbages and carrots, and human vomit. Hector cursed his poor fortune aloud as he shook his boot free, though in truth he could not have stank much more than he already did from his abattoir labors. Then Hector began to cry and for the rest of his life never knew why. The tears came so quickly that he took them for rain, just as he took the shaking sobs of his body for the buffeting of the wind. One could speculate that it was at this moment that Hector realized that his life was a very bad dog that would never obey him and now and then bit him and would one day catch him by the throat and be done with him. Hector consoled himself on the rest of the wet walk with a waking dream of Francoise in their new home with a steaming cup of tea she was setting just now on the table to await his return.

THE NEXT DAY, HECTOR, having determined that there was no wind, palmed the pinch of powder, purchased fruit, and lightly let fall the magic on the hair of Francoise as she looked down for a torn page of newspaper in which to wrap this unknown customer's cherries. As he released the powder, Hector recited the words given to him by the magus, the meaning of which he did not comprehend beyond that they would win her heart. For a few moments, as he strolled down the Rue du Fauborg eating ripe cherries and spitting pits, Hector was certain that this woman of red hair and red heart and red loins—he pulsed as he thought of her—would not only be his but would thank him for having redeemed her from a life of loveless solitude. As for the abattoir, Hector did not intend to remain there much longer. His plan was to serve as the chosen apprentice of Stanislaus and learn from him the spells that could master life.

THE FURTIVE WOMAN who had passed by Hector on the stairway to the chambers of the magus Stanislaus was of course Francoise, who had veiled herself so as not to be seen and had no idea, as she eyeballed Hector through her lace, who on earth he was or why he had preceded her to the dark chamber above. Her own purpose was to gain the aid of Stanislaus in driving the devil out of her two eldest, Gabriel and Gabrielle, for their ceaseless acts of cruelty were turning the youngest, Marguerite, ever more pale. Francoise had brought the local priest to their home but his exorcisms had only prompted the two possessed ones to laugh. Stanislaus saw her in and provided her with a jar of potion that she was to rub into the backs of the necks of the two each night at bedtime for a week. He assured her that this blessed potion contained the pulverized feather from a holy angel's wing and the distillation of a dozen tongues of doves. The payment he suggested and received was the sexual favors of Francoise, who was happy to provide them instead of cash, for which she had far greater need than for an hour of her evening which would otherwise have been devoted to holding poor Marguerite's head in her lap so as to compel the two possessed ones to drive Grandmama amok instead. Let Grandmama, who ate for two, tend all three tonight. As for Stanislaus, the pleasures he now attained were precisely those which Hector had beseeched just a half hour prior. It was, without Stanislaus knowing it, the culmination of his magical career.

ONE OF THE READERS of *When to Go into the Water* was a woman who enjoyed reading in public because her private life had become a horror. The few lovers she had allowed to touch her in her twenty-some years had left violent marks on her body, as had her father before them. Her body now preferred to live in her mind while it read books that told stories that had nothing to do with her own. She read in coffeehouses. While she read in her apartment in which she lived alone she would grow afraid that someone from her past would knock on the door and ask for another chance. She was out of chances, even for herself. Her mind was an overcharged battery that needed draining—which was what the books did, their texts running themselves silly in her head. But when she tried to read alone in her apartment her body, fearing that knock, gave way and tried to die so that the book could be even better without her. When she read in public she became part of a bigger something that couldn't all be sucked into the book she alone was holding and reading. An occasional sip from her coffee—no milk, no cream, no sugar, no nothing—she wanted to show the customers and staff that she was still there just as much as they were. She wears no ring, she gets hit on by women and men alike who can't figure out if she's ever decided. What she is now is celibate. What she wants now is never to have sex again. The few times in her life that she came were with men and at those times, at the peak, the height, she fantasized herself racing around trying to find a door to the room into which she could go and never know or care ever again what was happening outside that door. She read *When to Go into the Water* one night in a Starbucks and poured the glass of water that the waitperson had brought with her coffee over her own head in response to the book's admonition: "There is no prison so vast, so various in its tortures, as our own memories. Can we ever hope to be pardoned and released? But then, to whom are we pleading? We are the wardens of our own prisons. Wash the grime of the past from your skin and stand free in the present that is yours alone to live." The woman who loved to read let the water drip down her. The waitperson brought her a towel and asked if everything was OK. Inside herself the woman felt the water flowing into the cataracts of her heart.

FRANCOISE DID NOT FALL IN LOVE with Hector. Nothing at all changed the next several times he bought fruit. Stanislaus had warned him the only way the powder could fail was if Hector recited the spell without a steadfast focus. Hector was now left anguished. He began to imagine Francoise had somehow noticed him casting the powder upon her hair and, to taunt him, had resolved to ignore him all the more. There was no longer anything to hold him in Paris — not the abattoir, and certainly not the hope of an apprenticeship with Stanislaus, for how could Hector hope to be accepted by the magus after having bungled so badly his first magical outing? It was plain that, if he possessed a vocation, it was neither the occult nor the art of courtship. It also seemed plain that he needed to leave Paris, the setting of his failures, for a city in which no one knew him and he no longer knew himself.

WHILE CROSSING FROM CALAIS TO DOVER—there to find a train to London—Hector stood at the railing of the topmost deck of the ferry and stared out for the first time in his life at the vastness of the open seas. The weather was foul. The ferry pitched. Hector was steadfast, breathing in the beating salt air and feeling himself, for a few moments, captain of his fate. To celebrate, he went below and treated himself to a brandy in the ferry's saloon. As he stood and sipped, he was offered a cigarette by a comely Englishwoman whose husband promptly came to fetch her away after first accusing her, before Hector, of lewd drunkenness in casting her eyes at a ruffian who was scarcely more than a boy. Hector was so thrilled by it all that he immediately took up the habit of smoking, beginning with his consumption of madam's lipstick-ringed cigarette to the very tip.

IN LONDON, HECTOR FOUND shelter in a claptrap boarding house and ill-paid employment as a dishwasher in a Bloomsbury pub, The Midshipman's Watch. In the scullery, elbow-to-elbow with his native-born fellow workers, Hector found himself, within two months, not only able to converse in English but also to imitate various London upper- and lower-class accents with panache. The owner of the pub, overhearing this, promoted Hector to the far more prestigious but scarcely better-paid position of barman, where his skill at mimicry would enliven the customers and spur their thirst. The owner set aside a portion of Hector's salary toward the purchase of a suitable barman's wardrobe—pleated black pants, white pinstriped shirts, black bow tie, plaid suspenders, spiff black shoes. It was stipulated that Hector was to bathe once a week. With the tips he could expect to receive from the gents who frequented The Midshipman's Watch, it was further stipulated that he would acquire a flat in which he could bathe in private, rather than seeking out public facilities in which all manner of vice was rampant.

ONE OF THE READERS OF *When to Go into the Water* was a fading male movie star of the 1990s, You Know Who. He happened to find a copy of Hector's book on the common-reader shelf of the tea room of a Carmel coastal bed-and-breakfast in which he had stayed for much needed rest after his latest film, *Jammed Drawers,* opened to hellacious reviews. In it, You Know Who played a psychopathic hit man who can empathize only with furniture, which he admires for its patience with people. This schizoid empathic streak gets in the way of his work. In one scene, he's got the contract victim between his crosshairs but won't squeeze the trigger because if he misses he takes out a lushly carved mahogany desk. But then he meets a woman who likes furniture even more than he does. She's an antique dealer, and she convinces him that bullet holes would only increase the value of fine furniture by adding a colorful history to its otherwise staid provenance. As for cheap furniture, why not put it out of its misery before it's donated to a thrift shop and purchased by a college kid who paints it purple? All this frees up the killer inside himself, but by now his mob boss employer thinks he's unreliably nuts and has him killed by a hit man disguised as a hutch. You Know Who had known from the start that the script was iffy, but it had been years since he had been offered anything other than iffy scripts. He now feared that *Jammed Drawers* would stop even those from arriving. That night, under his quilt with just his head and hands peeping out, he read in Hector's book: "For those few of us who pursue only what we love—a person, a vocation, are they not in essence one?—it is folly to expect that the crowds who pass us in the streets and share our train compartments will admire our devotion unless it has also brought us visible profit. It is permitted to draw shut the curtains of one's soul when such coin-counters approach. And if this means a return to solitude, remember this also—from the despair of solitude arises the strength to seek out new loves to which we can devote ourselves entire." You Know Who stopped reading at this point, shut off the light and drifted to sleep. He woke up refreshed, returned that same day to Los Angeles, and in his next round of publicity interviews for *Jammed Drawers* made a point, when talking to the reporter from a zine called *Cult Trash,* of giving credit to Hector de Saint-Aureole and his little book for opening up his heart to the truth that critics are like sad perverts who peek through the curtains of art into the actor's soul and pronounce it good or bad, entertaining or not—but never discern the emanating love.

HECTOR FOUND A FURNISHED FLAT with heated water provided. But now that he could afford the pittance to enter the public baths, and now that he had been made aware of the possibilities, Hector decided to take a plunge or two on his off Sundays. Outside the doors were men who served as procurers of women, within were younger men who for a fee procured themselves. Hector's own preference was for a lady of the night who was redheaded, like Francoise, but looked at Hector straight on and smiled at him as she undressed before him. To her his virginity toppled again and again at the age of nineteen. It was a joke between them, based on the fact that it was true, that he was falling in love with her. She would laugh and yank at his ear and tell him to stop spending his money on her when he should be saving for a wife. Hector relished his public bath afterwards, soaking in the warmth of the pool in which men such as himself postcoitally gathered for cleansing. Some smoked cigars that they ashed in bronze urns supplied for the purpose. Some read the speculations in the dailies on Home Rule for Ireland and the need for a reinvigorated Evangelicalism; during their bathing they glowed sanguinely regardless of the news they read, artfully holding the newsprint pages just above the froth of the soapy water. There was a smaller, colder pool in which to rinse afterwards. A towel was provided by a blind man whom one tipped a pence or two. And then Hector returned to his flat, where, in a notebook he kept in the sole drawer of a small oak desk, he began the habit of writing down—in English, the language in which he now lived—a sentence or so nearly every evening, as a sort of vespers, though he believed in little but love and in nothing so little as what he wrote.

ONE OF THE LONGTIME PATRONS of The Midshipman's Watch was a Scotsman employed in the archives of the British Museum. His name was Muir, he brooked no other, and in his youth he had earned a bachelor's in the classics at St. Andrews, where he studied under John Burnet, a famed scholar of Pre-Socratic philosophy who succeeded in conveying his passion for this field to Muir. In particular, Muir revered Heraclitus. Moisture, Muir took to telling Hector as Hector filled Muir's pint of bitter to the overflowing brim, moisture in the body was the source of sound sleep and the earmark of intense pleasure. The moist and the fiery contended within us, both essential to life. But fire alone could bestow the higher life of the spirit, if only men could but learn to enable the fire to burn, to rise, to triumph. Moisture, the alluring mist that clouded brains and engorged loins, moisture in the ascendant ate at the fire. And moisture in its full drunken surge—here Muir's eyes after his fifth pint raged—turned the fire to ashes. How else explain the allure of a pub to men upon the finish of their day, Muir asked, if not as a means of extinguishing for a precious while the soul's somber vision of the truth? Hector nodded in agreement with this freckled, middle-aged man who was generous with his gratuities. Muir began, in the way of a bachelor with adequate means and an unfulfilled heart, to take the liberty of regarding Hector the barman as something of a son.

"THE DROWNING MAN LOOKS upon water as the source of his doom," Hector wrote late that night. "The parched man sees it as the source of life. Water itself is without desire and washes all philosophies away."

HECTOR FOUND HIMSELF at Muir's house on a late summer Sunday night. There was one other guest to complete the threesome, a friend of Muir's from their days at St. Andrew's. His name was Edward, his cheekbones bulged beneath gaunt eyes, and his head was utterly bald but for behind-the-ears grey tufts that seemed all the more forlorn for having survived in such isolation. Edward had also studied the Pre-Socratics under Burnet, but his view of their worth was altogether different from that of Muir. It's bloody poetry is all and poor poetry at that, and not a one of their fragmented riddles on moisture and dryness can help you to pass through a day of life's allotted grief, was the gist of what Edward muttered on about. Unlike Muir, who had turned to brandy, Edward's beverage of choice was a sober pear nectar. Hector sipped a stout. When asked by Muir what he thought of Edward's remarks, Hector understood that he was now expected to show how he had benefited from Muir's nightly bar-rail tutorials on Heraclitus as Hector poured him his bitters. The more trusting, not to say intimate, Muir's regard for Hector became, the less he spoke to the young man of anything other than Greek philosophy. Hector now said to Edward: "What better guide and solace for a weary day of life than Heraclitus's maxim: 'You cannot step twice into the same rivers; for fresh waters are ever flowing in upon you.'" Edward merely yawned at Hector's recitation, but Muir frowned, taking it as a warning against seeking to bathe a second time in the waters of youth. Hector was pleased that he had gotten the quote off correctly and helped himself to a slice of stilton on a biscuit. Back at his flat later that night, as he smoked a Player's cigarette that he ashed in a sardine tin left over from a long ago meal, Hector wrote: "I am as grand and compliant a whore as my red-headed London mistress-

34

by-the-hour. Invite me to eat and to drink my fill and I will recite whatever my host desires. I am happy to do so. But how faint a happiness it is to be kind to one who loves you when you do not love in return. In the future, when my beloveds refuse me, I must remember that such kindnesses offer no solace worth having."

IT WAS NOT VERY LONG AFTER this that Muir ceased to appear in The Midshipman's Watch, and not very long after that a clerk from the offices of the solicitors Barclay and Harrap arrived in the pub and, rather than ordering a pint, handed Hector official notice of the need for his presence at the reading of the will of Barnabas Muir who had died 3 March 1924. As it happened, Muir had, when young, attained to a considerable family fortune and had gone on to invest it wisely in East India Company shares that burgeoned along with the British Empire. Muir had lived well but not lavishly, lived singly but not lasciviously, and had designated Hector to inherit the entirety of an estate that amounted to some £300,000 — a fortune to assure a lifetime of ease and choice. The will was read in a boardroom in which the solicitor Barclay, his obedient clerk, and a delirious Hector were the only persons in attendance. When Barclay offered him a fine quill pen with which to sign the parchments of transfer, Hector felt himself at once grow accustomed to wealth.

THE OWNER OF THE MIDSHIPMAN'S WATCH rued the fortune that might have been his had he and not Hector become the confidant for a surreptitiously rich old soak's philosophic musings on moisture. But the owner had no wish to antagonize a newly minted gentleman of means and resolved to throw his departing barman a goodwill sendoff celebration. In the wee hours after closing on the Saturday night that followed the reading of the will, the owner and his staff toasted Hector again and again. When all were in their cups — a state decried by Heraclitus as parlous for those who would retain their hard-won wisdom — a speech was urged of Hector, for to a soul they wondered what they would do were they in Hector's place, and so they craved the details of how he planned to proceed to please and perhaps deprave himself. Hector, dressed in a newly acquired tweed suit and plus fours, had been served copious pints that night by the owner himself who, in the spirit of the occasion, had dressed down in a barman's uniform. Hector now wobbled to the end of the bar, grasped its brass rail, hoisted himself to a seated position on the shining teak counter, eyed about him the gas chandeliers that were reflected multifold in the wall mirrors mingled with hanging portraits of Lords Nelson and Byron, of Chinese Gordon and Jenny Lind, and at last betook himself and addressed the crew of The Midshipman's Watch in a voice so soft it required some seconds for them to discern that the Hector they had been raucously toasting was leaving them behind without the slightest regret: "I want to do everything I haven't yet dared to do, and to escape everything I've already done. I want to die in a cataclysm of my own making, not in a world war fashioned by great nations. And I want to leave a written record of my passage across this earth, so that others who find it elusive to taste what they desire can know, at least, that I too have searched in vain before them." Not a word addressed to his fellow workers, no nostalgia for the push-and-shove in the scullery during his dishwashing days, no funny yarns about serving the drunken regulars. The celebration broke up shortly afterwards, with Hector being shown the door by the owner who thought to himself that the reward for giving work to a poor French frog was to be high-hatted when the frog made good. Hector found himself on the cold foggy street that, in his inebriation, seemed a stage setting for the start of mysterious adventures. He hailed a hansom cab and, when he arrived at his new digs at the posh Hotel Russell, he tipped the cabman some pence more than the norm and received an ardent good morning in return.

"I HAVE MADE A COMPLETE ass of myself by baring my soul to my fellow men after having sluiced pints of bitter down my garrulous throat," Hector wrote before falling into bed that night. "Henceforth my mode of operation will be to keep myself to myself so far as possible—that self-enforced exile will end only with the arrival into my life of my true beloved, should that ever come to be. In the interim, while walking and talking in the world, I shall act in accordance with the customs and desires of those around me— until I see my chance for escape. Escape to where? I shall travel the globe to determine the possibilities, or perhaps to conclude instead that the prison is perfectly constructed. And to whom can I now confide all this but to my future readers, who will by virtue of scanning my words and not my face make of me their perplexing friend and not the ready fiend they would espy, if authors were truly on view in their own pages, scribbling in haste in the dark by the glow of cigarette after cigarette, each lit in turn by the last."

ACCORDING TO THE SOLICITOR BARCLAY, Muir had specified in his last will and testament that, while his house and the chattel therein could be sold if Hector wished—which Hector did wish, having no desire to live in the pervasive shadow of his benefactor—Muir's personal library was to be "kept intact and thereafter to be consulted attentively by my sole heir." Hector inquired of Barclay as to the penalty for breaching this clause and saw the solicitor's brows raise as if the top of his head had been tapped upon. By an angel or a devil, Hector wondered, but Barclay's brows had lowered again and the entire gesture passed into metaphysics of a sort for which neither man cared. "Penalty there is none," Barclay explained. "The deceased chose to employ an ethical admonition to be obeyed for its own sake." "Well, Barclay, we are all fond of making ethical admonitions, are we not?" "We are," Barclay consented. Hector went to Muir's home that evening and made a thorough examination of the library, which was dedicated strictly to two fields—the Greek and Roman classics, and erotica from anywhere Muir could get it. Hector spent the night in Muir's favorite armchair sampling the deceased's fine brandies and perusing privately printed editions that pictured and textually elaborated upon the ranges of sexual pleasure from courtship to copulation with all manner of partners in diverse lands and times including, by sheerest artistic license, the Pleistocene. Few of the artists and authors dared name themselves, though they dared everything else. Volume after volume did Hector consume with ocular wonder, the fumes from the brandies serving as incense for the debauch. At last, tucked at the end of a high shelf, Hector discovered a book that in width and heft was scarcely a book at all. The cover was of silk the color of red rose petals long pressed between the pages of a book, the spine was of virginal calf-leather upon which was embossed, in tiny gold-leaf Gothic letters, *The Proper Tutoring of the Barman*. The first page was devoted to an epigram from the Roman poet Juvenal, a name Hector remembered from those occasions when Muir in his cups would caterwaul some bits of Latin verse. The text set forth here was in English, and it dawned at once upon Hector, despite the alcohol swirling in his head, that the choice of English over the Latin original had been made for the sake of himself, Hector, the long-intended reader: "Destiny governs man; it influences the parts that the toga covers. If your star pales, useless will be the length and strength of your member to you—even though Virro shall have seen you naked with lips that water." The contents of the book proper were limited to two prints, each hand-colored on the finest vellum. The first, entitled "The Tutor's Lament," portrayed a slim boyish man in pleated black trousers bending over, face hidden, to fetch ale bottles while a freckled, middle-aged man sits at the bar with the sadness a teacher might show at a student's disinterest. The second print, "The Tutor's Delight," transported the younger and older man from the bar to a new setting, a book-lined room that was the very room in which Hector now sat staring at the depiction of his own face aglow from the lesson provided by Muir, whose glee left no doubt that he had, Juvenal be damned, triumphed over destiny with a flourish. A book made to order at Muir's direction, to which Muir's last testament had directed his legatee. Hector added it up: Muir, lacking both physical capability and any real hope of having his affections returned, had chosen Hector as his heir so as to bestow upon him the only form of love he could. For the first time, as he sat with the two prints before him, he wept for Muir's death. Hector now knew

41

himself to be, by their shared devotion to the secret desires of the heart, Muir's brother. The next day, Hector summoned the most eminent book dealer in London to the house and sold off to him all of the books devoted to the Greeks and the Romans. The book dealer would have preferred to purchase the collection of erotica, which, he averred, would be worth far more. But Hector chose instead to ship these en masse—with one exception—to Barclay's offices, by way of concluding their talk on ethical admonitions. As for *The Proper Tutoring of the Barman*, he consigned it to a safety deposit box in a bank just off Piccadilly Circus, his feeling being, as he made the arrangements, that he did not wish to carry the book along on his travels nor to part forever with it, so why not keep it safe somewhere and come back someday for a sentimental visit. As soon as Hector left the bank, he realized that he would never return, that his feelings for Muir had had their time. Eighty years later, in 2004, the box, deemed abandoned, was opened by a bank employee who slipped the book under his vest and promptly sold it on the Internet as vintage Edwardian porn to a wealthy gay collector who came to include the unknown young barman, whom he called "Virro," in his own fantasies of moist lips.

ONE OF THE READERS OF *When to Go into the Water* was a former UFO abductee named Claude who played five hours with breaks on the hour six nights a week in a piano bar in Little Rock, Arkansas, and loved his work and the people who sat to listen to him play so much that, having made it to his fifties and survived so many years of blistering failure—including marriage to a woman who came to prefer her own gender; marriage to a woman who left him for a younger pony-tailed pianist in Austin, Texas; marriage to a woman who could not keep her balance and fell into a wishing well that became, after her much-publicized drowning death, closed to the general public; and marriage to a woman who poured concrete over the keys of his piano because she could not stand him singing lovelorn ballads once she'd learned what a morose self-absorbed asinine bastard he really was—Claude had, in his own view, become the luckiest person on the face of the earth. He lived alone, rented cheap, slept late, got free drinks on the job so long as his playing didn't sound sloshed, which it never did, for Claude possessed a true ease at the keys. Regulars tipped him well for playing their favorites over and over again and applauded his flourishes and his pinky-finger arpeggios. His voice, which was low and slow and soft and sad and smooth, was holding out. Now and then the ladies still liked to try him out, and when they didn't, he had more room in the bed and far more peaceful mornings. So one night, Claude has just finished a run of "Lost Highway," "It Could Happen to You," and "It's Only a Paper Moon," because the man's got the chops and range to please his high-octane clientele, and on his break he steps outside his club, The Splash, a name Claude likes as it suggests a wildness Claude thinks he can still muster in his songs. Claude is trying to give up smoking and trying not to want a cigarette makes

43

him think of Hector de Saint-Aureole, that crazy rich guy who wrote by the beady red light of his smokes. The wife who had made his keyboard a rock-hard gray slab loved that book of his and used to read it out loud to Claude to prove that men could be sensitive. Claude's own personal view about water was that Hector should have just shut up and dived in. Hell. It was all over soon enough anyhow. Claude looks up at the night sky and sees that silly paper moon he'd just been singing about and then he sees a beam of pink light as rich and wavy as the frosting on one of his wedding cakes. That was it for a while. When Claude awoke he was seated in a kind of chair that was more like an expansive plasma adjusting itself to his every movement and devoting itself to his comfort. Opposite Claude, in a similar plasma chair, was what looked like a squid with the head of a young dappled deer and a screen in its chest that flashed English-language queries and responses that allowed Claude and the alien to converse. The alien explained that the thought-recording apparatus of the scanning mother ship had detected in Claude the conviction that his luck exceeded that of all his fellow humanoids. That made Claude worthy of questioning, as the aliens planned to colonize earth and raise and eat humans and needed to know how to keep them content so that the taste of their innards stayed succulent as they fed and grew fat. What is luck? asked the screen. Not wanting more than you already got, Claude responded, but if you really want to understand us earthlings, put me back at my piano and then request a song—if you're embarrassed to show your screen in public, you can shoot the title into my head with that pink beam, right? You come up with a song that I can sing and I'll know you're reading me right. And then sit there at the bar and have a drink and maybe flirt with the lady

44

beside you. You'll find out all you'll need to know about humans and how we all live and what our brains will be thinking while you're sucking them out through our ears. "Sounds like a hoot and a holler" appeared on the screen in the alien's chest along with a smiley face. It could have been a second or a year later—the molecular decomposition and recomposition of his teleported body having dulled his time sense, though he saw at once that he hadn't been missed at The Splash—that Claude was back before the ivories and a young man with the most sensitive eyes and what seemed to be numerous excess arms tucked into his jacket requested "Send in the Clowns" and, after beaming the bartender to set up a series of straight-up shots of Wild Turkey, struck up a gestural conversation with a woman who moved away from him because she thought he was some kind of pathetic freak, which the alien picked up on not through his pink beam but through the stronger message of her eyes narrowed and flaming with scorn. The alien suddenly realized that, if pretending to be human was hard, being human must be even harder, and all that pain would seep into their innards no matter how luckily they were raised. But the alien hung with Claude's yearning set all the way through "Night and Day," "Look What Thoughts Can Do," and, most devastating, "Stardust," during which the alien wept outright. Come closing time, the alien left in wobbly despair, unaccustomed as he was to human passion and human loss. He won't be back, Claude thought to himself, let some other species on some other planet have its brains sucked out dry. A newly powerful thirst persuaded Claude, as he appeased it, to keep his UFO abduction to himself or people would want to hear about that instead of listen to his songs, and then his luck that even the aliens could sense would be over for good.

HECTOR DECIDED THAT HE WOULD ATTEND a theatre performance, for he had heard a good deal about the theatre and had passed by many a West End marquee with their posters of dapper tuxedoed men and soignée women in graceful evening dresses draped tantalizingly over their impossibly supple bodies. Realizing that he wanted to look at the beautiful people who made their living onstage and was not at all interested in having them act out an ambitious drama, he purchased a private box from which to witness a dance hall revue that was billed as the finest in London. Bathed and attired in his formal best, Hector brought along a pair of opera glasses and arranged for champagne and oysters on ice to be brought and served to him a quarter of an hour prior to the rising of the curtain. Drinking and eating and viewing the audience through his glasses, Hector observed that the men and the women alike were flushed and excited. Hector was of course observed in return, and in particular by a short woman with raven-black hair, plucked eyebrows, beestung lips, and a body nowise delicate but rather fulsome and then some. This woman was the featured headliner performer whose image on the posters plastered across London had caught the attention of Hector each time he had passed them or rather her by. She was now dancing a dance that had become the publicized craze of the season. It was called the "Black Bottom" and she danced it in a short silken silver-beaded dress that scarcely concealed black stockings rising to the crests of her buttocks, which she shook in manners both slow and sudden. The woman could not help but notice Hector, as he was leaning out of his box with his opera glasses crushed against his eyes. He was, she surmised as she danced the "Black Bottom," the sort of man so unused to opera glasses that he believed himself invisible while he

spied through them upon the world. She smiled at him and gave
him a wink and he thereupon fell back so clumsily that he tipped
the iced champagne onto the table of iced oysters, all of which now
splashed upon his shirtfront and face. It occurred to her, as she
took her bows and acknowledged the standing cheering whistling
clapping audience, that the man would have to be rich to be so
stupid. But that was harsh—was it not perhaps, rather than
stupidity, a coddled inexperience that could pleasantly be
remedied? It was a question of some import, as she expected to
receive his card as she changed in her dressing room after the show,
and she decided that yes she would see him for he was young and
so few rich men were.

A HECTOR DE SAINT-AUREOLE wishing to see Carrie Pennington, the vest-pocket beauty of the season. Carrie instructed her dresser to keep him waiting five minutes and then let him in. She gazed into her brightly lit dressing-room mirror, removing with daubs of cream the pink highlights painted onto her cheeks and the sparkling blue that coated her eyelids and the kohl underscoring that gave to her eyes the fervid passion requisite for her dance. What was left was a face of simple sensuous beauty. Her silver dress was hanging upon a Japanese silk-screen partition from which, in exchange, she now plucked the violet robe in which she was accustomed to greet backstage admirers, realizing full well that a glimpse of her in so intimate a garb encouraged their most heated declarations of passion. She relished these declarations, for after all, from their lot would come her future husband, and until then she was entitled to some spoils, was she not? Her dresser at last informed Hector that he could enter, and as he turned the knob of the door he fought off a dizzying spinning within his head that could have left him prostrate, had he not the determination to make of this moment all that he could. Carrie Pennington, still in her black stockings, gazed upon the latest entrant. A weakened Hector grasped the back of an armchair placed for visitors such as himself, bowed awkwardly from the waist, and whispered, "Mademoiselle, I plead with you, teach me how to dance with the abandon and joy you bring to the stage," and promptly fainted. Carrie rang for her dresser who brought salts.

HECTOR CROSSED THE ATLANTIC TO AMERICA in a first-class suite on a Cunard liner and had a shipboard romance with a lovely young lady whose gambling debts in the ship's casino Hector settled discreetly. His own behavior in the affair, which amounted to paying tacitly for sex with a languid unheeding ingénue, disgusted him. When the liner docked in New York, Hector promptly fled the city and its temptations for the unpopulated purity of the far north. He discovered one day, during a downpour in Manchester, Vermont, to which he had come to witness the legendary autumn colors, that within him dwelled a horror of standing beside gushing rainspouts and gulping gutters, of bearing witness to water rush away to the bowels of the earth. In the coolness of the heavens that follows so vehement a weeping, there remained, for Hector, a stench rising from the soil as of too much drinking, rank as the pools of spilled bitter he'd swabbed nightly off the floors of The Midshipman's Watch. Hector returned to his stately white-pillared New England inn, phoned down from his room to instruct that brandy and soda and ice and sliced pears with bleu cheese and a rosemary-roasted chicken with yams and peas and cloverleaf rolls and balls of freshly churned butter and a pumpkin pie with whipped cream be brought him. He then changed into his silken Turkish dressing gown striped vertically red and green, and tipped the bellhop liberally upon the arrival of his dinner on a cart with a cream-colored table cloth and napkin and a setting of Chinese porcelain and sterling silver. Seated upon his bed he gorged. The food sufficiently absorbed the brandy so that his state, when he collapsed into sleep, was less that of drunkenness than of a newly acute awareness of the difficulty of breathing with one's eyes open, and of the astonishing new world that opened out once they closed. Upon awakening the next

49

morning, Hector could only recall that in his dream he was conversing once more with Stanislaus, the magus of Paris, who now advised Hector that bathing was a cure for pain and that weeping in the bath was all the better. So Hector bathed and wept and went out again into the world to see the colors on the beetling hillsides — red and yellow and orange and not at all green on this sunny blue day on which Hector felt consciously his youth end.

Hector de Saint-Aureole, circa 1927.

HECTOR WAS NOW DRAWN to cold and unvisited far northern lakes. His guide on this occasion was a French-Canadian descendant of the voyageurs, with whom Hector allowed himself the indulgence of speaking the language of his youth. Perhaps as a result, Hector became something of a boy enthralled by the tales told by Pierre the guide as he manned the rear steering paddle of their canoe, leaving Hector the less complicated task of bow stroking in obedient rhythm. They set up camp in the eastern cove of a shimmering lake the shape of a scimitar. As the campfire blazed, Pierre—whose greased black mustache shone and whose eyes were as slitted as a lizard's from decades of exposure to the glare of sun on water—related to Hector a legend that once a man had lived alone beside this lake, a man who had been forsaken in love and resolved to forsake life in return. To here he came, built himself a small cabin—there, you can see its remains half-hidden in the trees on the opposite shore; it has fallen apart of its own in the rains and snows that have come since the man, one midnight, betook himself in his canoe to the middle of the lake, laid his paddle across the thwarts, and asked the moon, the stars, the trees, and the water that were his only remaining company if it would be rudeness on his part to end his stay among them, for he could not forget the woman to whom he had offered a life of peace along this lake on which their children would paddle and swim and fish while they two watched from their cabin, which he would construct to her wishes. As he waited for her response, a smile played across her face and then she laughed outright. Now, to comfort the man, the moon caressed his heated brow and the stars brushed out his long unbarbered hair and the trees fanned forth a gentle wind but the water only stared back at him and showed him himself in the moonlight, a man with a face like a bootprint, seated in a canoe that he could paddle back to his solitude—or not. According to Pierre, there were two variant endings to the legend. In one, the man then resolved to slip from the canoe into the water and was never found, though his ghost can be seen hovering at that very spot in the midst in the lake when the moon is full as it is tonight, can't you see him? In the other ending, he paddles to shore, makes his way back to the cities of men, forgets everything he has seen and known, gets a job he doesn't like, a wife he doesn't love, a religion he doesn't believe, and a son he beats— until one day, all grown, the son guides the aging father here and drowns him in this lake which the father had abandoned but never ceased to speak of as his lost paradise. The son, then, Hector asked, acted out of filial piety and made both versions of the legend true in essence? Pierre doffed his red cap and smiled, the moonlight bathing his brow, the stars braiding his hair.

IN THE WOODS, BEWILDERED, in a peck of troubles, at a loss. To ascend a pulpit, to cant, to remove one's vestments with one's teeth, to chase foxes at clicket in a hedge, to stand stooped in the pillory, cunny-thumbed, one who has eaten shame and drank a dram after it. Woodpeckers crying peccavi and tearing at the pillory bonds. The blowen has napped the scold's cure. To scour or score off, to run away, whittling the scrap, an old dance to a quick movement, thin legs like sticks with which small boys play swords. Riotous bucks giving way in the woods to wendigos feet on fire touching bone and whistle. The cove carries the cag. Totty-headed hats composed of diverse animals formerly worn by women to stiffen the foreparts of their stays, provoking the crime of bugging or stealing the beaver while weaving in lesser furs. Sights; anything to feed the eye. Come abroad for a little gapeseed. Counterfeit sleep to decoy prey. Say you bought your beef of me said the butcher to the fat man who flared. To be reduced to one's shifts, betraying oneself out of fear, hopper-arsed as the Devil in a high wind. Brimstone and milk. It derives its appellation from being hot in the mouth. The cull is leaky, and cackles; the rogue tells all out of distant hopes of preferment. I'll mill your glaze. It is all bob let us dub the gig of the case. Falling into a patch of ivy that excites an insufferable suffering. Vomiting. Waking in a sweat that turned instantly cold on his face. Hector reached for the scented handkerchief on his nightstand. Then, despite past warnings to himself against writing in the morning, he inscribed: "There is no more needful time for bathing than after a nightmare, for only the cool ubiquity of water on the skin convinces the body that the mind can be quelled."

ONE NIGHT IN FIJI, as Hector walked the beach, while overhead the shooting stars seemed to outnumber the stationary, his bare foot struck a cowrie shell lodged in the powdery sand. Could the two-lobed mollusk within it still be alive, Hector wondered, and wondered also if he should throw the beautiful ovoid shell back into the sea. Later that night, as he ashed his cigarette into the cowrie with its luscious daubs of amber and purple, Hector wrote: "There is no wet or dry, only wetter and drier, and in the far extremities lies oblivion. We are all destined to wash upon shores that seem as deserts to us and as pleasure beaches to those who abide there. Let us find the strength to walk those shores and parch the throat of death."

WHILE TRAVELING IN JAPAN, Hector was taken on a tour of an extensive holding of rice paddies. His host was the landowner, a bald florid farmer as prosperous as Hector's family had been poor. The landowner possessed a collection of rare netsuke pieces that Hector would be allowed to view at tour's end. The third member of their party was their translator, a geisha who noticed the lachrymose absence in Hector's eyes and suitably trimmed her employer's explanations of the challenges of tending rice. Chief among these challenges was adequate irrigation, and as to this point alone Hector posed a question or two as to depth and incline of the ditches. The dimensions are moderate as water is compliant, so the geisha explained in what Hector suspected were very much words of her own. Hector rephrased it to his own taste: water can be duped into anything. No shape or task outside the pale so long as a proper concavity and pressure are found. A slave to a rice farmer. Lubricant to the human body. An oceanic presence in which, at successive depths, the eaters and the eaten fatten and darken. Hector was at length ushered into the landowner's home. The collection was kept in glass-fronted lacquer cabinets with inset electric lighting that the owner now flicked on for all the cabinets at once. So numerous and intricately placed were the tiny carved ivory pieces that each cabinet seemed to Hector to hold a city unto itself, inhabited by ragged fishermen, round-bellied merchants, fierce samurai, famished demons, masked Noh actors, goddesses of mercy, wizened emperors, blossoming courtesans, oblivious buddhas, flinching servants, arrogant egrets, devoted dogs, laughing monkeys, braying donkeys, coiled dragons. The owner allowed Hector to hold one of the pieces—an old sorceress with a rotating ivory ball carved into her head that allowed Hector, with a flick of his thumb, to change her face from a deep-set skull to a rising smiling moon. What fascinated Hector was that the ivory felt unutterably dry upon his palm.

AN INTERNET BOOKSELLER DRESSED in a Liz Phair t-shirt and blue jeans stained by damp red streaks from the salsa of his morning omelet was browsing a rummage sale in Ely, Minnesota, for strange out-of-the-way crap he could mark up steeply as rarities. He came upon a copy of *When to Go into the Water* a trifle rubbed on the spine, title page inscribed by the author, "To my sure and eloquent guide Pierre, in remembrance of an unforgettable evening in the North, from a grateful Hector de Saint-Aureole." The bookseller had no idea who Saint-Aureole was, but he figured that an autographed copy of a finely bound obscurity should fetch something outlandish from some crazy person somewhere on the planet. So he bought it for fifty cents, took it home, checked the on-line listings and found no other copies of the book for sale. Sweet. Seller's market. He decided to price it at $175, adding this enticement to the standard condition-of-book details: "Poignant inscription to his friend (?) 'Pierre' assures the uniqueness of this rare copy of a work by an author distinguished in his vein." Whatever the fuck that vein may be, the bookseller muttered to himself as he threw the new listing out as raw bait in the digital waters. Two years later he marked it down to $6.00 for which it sold to someone who thought it was a bedwetting-prevention manual.

YOU KNOW WHO, FINISHED AT LAST with the dreadful publicity tour for his latest box-office bomb *Jammed Drawers*, had returned to his hideaway chateau in the Aleutian Islands. The first full day of blessed isolation he devoted to drinking heavily while watching the waves slap the cliff face that plunged from just below his bay window down into the depths of the Bering Strait. According to Saint-Aureole, You Know Who was thinking as the vodka hit, the cardinal rule is never go into the water if you're not sure you can get back out. So I shouldn't be thinking what I am thinking, that jumping into the sea would be easier for me than having to live through the death of my career. Just then, he heard a hearty three-beat knock on the door of his chateau. You Know Who was delighted to find that Bert the local bush pilot and postal carrier had landed with his weekly delivery. Aside from the usual catalogs, bills, and solicitations, there was a single letter addressed by hand to You Know Who care of the studio, which had forwarded it here. Time had been when Bert brought dozens of fan letters with each delivery. This was the first in three months. Wishing Bert a good day, You Know Who took care to close the door gently so as to mask his intense excitement over the heartfelt praise that he could already feel pulsing through the envelope into his fingers. Ripping it open, he read a handwritten note signed by a Daphne de Saint-Aureole inquiring if, on the basis of his comments in *Cult Trash*, he might be interested in the film rights to her father's book, a project for which the Saint-Aureole estate had allocated funds, should his daughter, who was also his executrix, determine, in her sole discretion, that an actor of sufficient sensibility to do justice to a nonsolid theme could be found. His performance in *Jammed*

Drawers, she went on to say, had more than convinced her on that score. You Know Who dropped to his knees and whispered: "Sweet God Almighty, I'm back in the game."

NOT SINCE PARIS IN HIS YOUTH and his passion for Francoise had Hector tasted the love which unifies body and soul into an anguish of mystical sweetness. It happened once more while he was staying in a luxury Hong Kong hotel just off the Conduit Road, all suites and apartments stylishly furnished, cool, and very clean with electric lights and room-service bells, hot showers and baths and balcony vistas of the harbor and the tiered houses rising from the water's edge unto the surrounding hilltops. The British crown colony was flourishing, and Hector saw it as a place where a man of independent means could drink and converse and watch the peoples of the world go by, which suited him as he felt tired. Of what, he wondered, dressed in white evening jacket and black pants and tie, seated on the blue silken sheets of the vast bed with which his room was fitted, trying to rouse himself to go out to dinner rather than order in as he had been doing night after night. Was it possible that he was fated ever to be alone? It was at "this precise moment of abject ennui," as Hector later wrote, that he heard "a sobbing so passionate that it seemed capable of rending its victim apart. Out of pity, I threw open my door and espied hunched in the mirrored hallway a woman wrapped in a scarlet silken robe down which cascaded her raven hair. She now began to catch at her mouth with her hands so as, I gathered, not to create any more of a disturbance than she already had by drawing me out of my suite. She saw that I was watching her raptly and, in despair at having been caught out in her time of heartbreak, dropped her hands to her lap, revealing a long face with moon-ivory skin and frantic lapis eyes, and began to sob all the more. I observed in that moment the face of a woman whose anguish was her beauty and so she could not escape herself. She rose, caught her breath, and

61

continued down the hallway, disappearing rightward to a room which I was to learn was number 23. In the weeks to come, I would many times retrace her steps in my pilgrimages to that chamber, for I could not but adore a soul so afire that she wept without tears."

HECTOR HAD A NOTE DELIVERED to the sobbing lady, whose name, Elise Durst, he obtained from the hotel concierge who recognized her from Hector's description and was rewarded with the largest tip he had ever received in a lifetime of obsequious service—a tip sufficient to cover the costs of the Confucian temple observances for his father who had just passed on. Such was the merest ripple of Hector's newly flowing love. His note to her explained his status as a fellow hotel guest who had by chance observed her in her apparent grief the night before and stood ready to be of comfort and assistance. Might he suggest a trip together by the Peak Tramway—with its dramatic view of the harbor—to the Botanical Gardens with their terraces, slopes and parterres of blossoming flowers. Immersion in the beauties of nature is a solace to us all, is it not? And perhaps some refreshment afterwards at one of the harbor-side teahouses? Awaiting your word, I remain, Hector de Saint-Aureole. Having dispatched the note, Hector sat alone in his suite and awaited a reply. He remained there for three days, taking room-service meals but finding himself unable to summon the will to bathe or to remove his pajamas. He cursed himself for having dared to write to a woman who had shown how she despised him first by fleeing down the hallway and secondly by imprisoning him. On the morning of day four there arrived a note in the form of a page of prose torn from an unknown book; by virtue of meticulous crossing-out of all but five separated words on the page, the message read: "Flowers watered with tea fade." Hector lay helpless as tawdry tears fell to his pillow.

"A LESSER MAN SUCH AS MYSELF would have and did give up hope of ever touching the lady's heart," Hector later wrote. "But my despair was counteracted by the accident of our meeting in the lobby the very next day. I panicked but she smiled upon me and extended her arm. I took it, oh so gently, scarcely daring to believe she would not wrench it back from me in affront. And then she thanked me—in an ancient voice, in the voice we hear spoken to us in our dreams—for the kindness of my note without alluding to her own reply." Hector spent that afternoon walking about the hotel grounds with Elise, who was born in Manchuria of American Methodist missionary parents and had married, at age nineteen, a cad on leave from the British navy who had won her love by claiming to have been saved from sin by the example of her purity, and who proceeded to degrade her utterly, once they were wed, by drinking away their money and bringing whores home with him— whores with whom he invited Elise to join in shared debauch. In the ten years since their divorce, Elise had wandered the East Asian coast, earning her way as a teacher of English. She had renounced religion as lies told to children to shield them from the world, and her parents in turn renounced her. At present, Elise was the kept mistress of a married man who paid for her suite at the hotel as it suited him as a locale for their intermittent trysts. Hector craved to know more but all Elise would say was that he was handsome and enticingly insistent, came from a wealthy Hong Kong merchant family, had five children and was bored with the wife who had borne them, and kept several mistresses aside from Elise because he liked having as much and as different sex as he possibly could. Hector then asked how this made Elise feel and if it had perhaps been the cause of her sobbing? He was of course hoping she would declare herself ready to break away. But her response, as Hector recorded it, was only to the first of his questions and took no account of his heart: "When a woman and a man make love, they are the closest they can be together and the farthest they can be apart."

THEY PARTED THAT EVENING but had dinner the next. Over sautéed grouper with shaved papaya preceded by an eel soup, olives, cheeses, biscuits, and followed by crème de menthe, the two of them felt the sort of kinship growing which invites the brushing of each other's hands under the table. Candlelight flickered across the remains of their meal and Hector marveled at the delicate shell-shaped bites left by Elise in the biscuits as contrasted with the cobra thrusts that marked his own consumption style. They were in a silk-curtained teakwood booth in a restaurant Elise had recommended for its fidelity to the genuine Cantonese tradition; it was the favorite eating place of her lover, but this she did not tell Hector. In the midst of their meal, Hector whispered into her ear: "My dear one, I have yet to learn what caused you to weep so deeply the night I first saw you." For he hoped that she would tell of cruelties by her lover from which Hector could promptly swear to free her, would she but travel the world with him. She took his face in her hands which were as dry as ivory. "I wept," Elise said, "because my lover had told me that his son was dying of a malarial fever. I wept because, the night he told me that, for the first and only time he slept the night through with me and only wanted me to hold him and never once became aroused. I wept because I know that will never happen again and yet I remain content with him, which makes me an adulteress and a whore." "You are neither," Hector insisted, kissing her full on the mouth for the first time. He then added, in a hiss in which the crème de menthe had its way with him: "And if you are both, then I shall confine your sins and purchase your nights forever onwards." This was the evening of the Black Friday of 1929 that engulfed the stock markets of the world, and as they dined Hector's munificent stock portfolio was

66

well on the way to being zeroed out. His piles of bonds were largely intact, so he could still do what he wanted while most of the rest of the people in the world could not then or ever.

ONE OF THE READERS OF *When to Go into the Water* was a young man in his twenties who had as yet decided upon nothing. He saw the book on the shelf of a Salvation Army thrift shop in which he liked to hunt for vintage clothes with a certain style, though just what style he couldn't say. The title caught his eye because it seemed so self-evidently stupid, so he bought Hector's book, which cost less than the azure rayon shirt he almost liked but ultimately couldn't help but pass on. That night, with nothing else to do, he started reading. The pinballing narrative of Saint-Aureole's smiles and sorrows reminded him so strongly of himself that it was as if he had purchased his own autobiography that he had neither written nor authorized. For the first time in his life he knew what he wanted. He promptly quit the most recent of his half-assed jobs—sales person at an aromatherapy shop in which he had learned that all human seeking of sensuous cures is laden with lust and deceit—and fulfilled a recurring daydream of his boyhood that he had long remembered and never understood. In the daydream he had, staff in hand, climbed the conical path of a great mountain and fallen to his knees when he reached the top. He realized now that the daydream had presaged his monastic vocation, to be fulfilled in a mountainous clime. After some internet research, he decided to visit the idiorrhythmic monks of Mount Athos in Greece, whose sense of adventurous discipline appealed to him. When he arrived, he saw the mountain in his dream. His fervor was so evident that he was at once accepted as a novice. Three years later he took full monastic vows which extolled the freedom of obedience and the love that in mountainous solitude enflames the soul. The love did indeed enflame him, but it wasn't the love of God; it was the love of silence, of focused labor, of shared meals and prayers, of the scent of hyacinth which he now knew to be the antidote to sorrow, of days so alike that one no longer needed to count them by month or year. He was so happy that his obedience became perfect, and he always thanked whoever God might be for everything. Close to his death in his isolated cell he lay on his plank with a rough woolen blanket over his heaving chest and cried out to on high, "In this life You've given me heaven—so now let me die and be gone!"

ELISE WOULD NOT LEAVE HER LOVER. She had no desire to travel the world with Hector. From her perspective, there was no difficulty in having both men come to her room, for the man she loved had many women and no objection to her having other men so long as he never saw or knew of them. And Hector, did she not care for him only because he loved her so well? At this realization, she wept, then sought to comfort herself. After all, this Hector was no tragic figure. Did he not sport a straw hat and smoke his cigarettes in silence like all the other European men in Hong Kong? And she herself, was she not entitled to taste what life was like for her lover with his many mistresses by making of Hector her own conquest? So Hector suited her, especially as his ardor made him initially content with what little she could give. Weeks went by and Hector, now transformed from the weary man who had chosen Hong Kong for a drunken respite into a jazzed lover who couldn't get over his bad luck that a woman desperately in need of saving wouldn't allow him to take her out of this godforsaken harbor into which all the world's scum flowed to anywhere else she chose. What did she have to stay on for? In answer, he fantasized her lover, the Hong Kong merchant, as possessing rich black hair and limpid brown eyes and a belly that he patted with delight as she laid her head upon it and moved down. He tried to hide his jealousy from her, swore to himself each time he made his way to room 23 that it did not matter whether or not the "Do Not Disturb" sign hung upon the handle of her door. But Elise perceived that Hector, when he made love to her, was first and foremost overcoming the demon of the absent other lover. This left Elise feeling lonelier than ever. The last night she spent with Hector she asked if she could simply hold him, which Hector had taken as a sign that she was starting to love him. The next day a note was delivered to his suite that was composed in the same meticulous cross-out manner as the first she had sent him. This one read: "All touches travel too far. Now go." For thirteen days thereafter, Hector made his vigils to 23 morning, noon, and night and saw the same "Do Not Disturb" sign in place. Just once, on the thirteenth day, nearly midnight, he dared to disobey her and knock. Let her lover be there, let her spit in his face, he would declare himself one last time. The sound of his own breathing filled his ears as he waited in vain. The following day he left Hong Kong forever.

ON BOARD SHIP TO MADRAS, Hector became violently seasick. In the lassitudes that followed, Hector had mood and occasion to record observations like this: "Flotsam consists in all natural matter that floats upon the ocean. Jetsam consists in all manmade matter that floats upon the ocean. What then is a human corpse? And were I to slip myself over the side of the ship, would I possess the courage to let myself drown as flotsam drowns—nature blissfully sinking into itself—or would I start screaming for help as jetsam still claiming its right to salvation?" It was not the most buoyant of times for Hector, whose pain over the loss of Elise was mitigated only by bouts of exhaustingly dream-swirled sleep in which Elise slipped away again and again. When he did appear on deck or at meals, Hector cut a romantic figure among his fellow passengers on the luxury liner, with his taste for finely tailored evening wear, tall-stemmed martinis, and aromatic clove cigarettes, cartons of which he had purchased in Djakarta en route. But mostly Hector sat in his cabin and wrote stuff like this: "More and more it seems to me that I leave parts of me behind wherever I go. You might think that I should stop to pick them up, but as soon as I attempt to do so, they dissolve into realms that beckon like watery death."

THE DEVI, THE GODDESS OF GODDESSES, bestowed one of her engulfing visionary appearances upon Hector. It was during his visit to Benares, where he witnessed, at Mankarinka Ghat, the bathers in loincloths and turbans descending and ascending the vast stone-slab stairs as each took their turn at washing their souls in the Ganges. That evening, as Hector walked along the river, the Devi showed herself to him in the form of Lakshmi, the goddess of kind fortune. For Hector this was a rueful irony, coming as it did after Elise had already departed from his life. Lakshmi smiled and indicated by means of a subtle tip of the lotus she held like a scepter that Hector should be grateful it was she and not Durga the destroyer who had manifested to him on this teeming hot night. As they sat beside the river, Lakshmi recalled to Hector's eyes the time of her first arising, after the devas and asuras had churned the ocean to milk. Enthroned upon a floating lotus, her beauty was such that those who beheld her as Hector now did were released for a spell from the pain of living. Lakshmi ceased to reminisce and offered the rare praise, by a tilt of the head that set her dangling left earring of gold briefly singing, that Hector had no need to worship gods, for the gods had now twice in his life come of themselves to him, though not because he was particularly wise or kind, but rather because he asked for so little that a deity could converse with him with pleasure. But Lakshmi saw that Hector was wriggling inside his skin. No family, no friends, no regular human connections aside from small talk with bank tellers during currency exchanges. She bestowed upon Hector a vision of himself isolated in flames and in need of quenching. Hector supplicated the goddess by placing his head on her lap like a dog who knew he was hers. I shall fashion a means to lift your wandering loneliness, Lakshmi declared. But in

73

return I shall require a sacrifice—one of my choice, my time, my place. Be not one of those who seek to design their own sacrifice, Hector. Theirs is the falsehood of pride and the worship of pain. I am the ocean-born, trust in me, my every shade of meaning comes out in the wash and the poets find me pretty beyond words.

Laxumi (the Goddess of Wealth & Prosperity)

AS HE SAT OVER DRINKS in the Court of the Three Sisters in the French Quarter of New Orleans, You Know Who was wearing sunglasses to ward off the curious public that might still recognize him despite his recent string of box-office failures. Across the table from him, Hector's daughter, Daphne de Saint-Aureole—the first name her mother's choice, the last insisted upon by Hector despite her mother's refusal to marry—was nursing her glass of Sauvignon Blanc into which, on this steamy night, she had transferred the ice cubes that had come with her glass of water. Her long wavy brown hair framed a cheeky face with a small, sharp, sensuously nostrilled nose and pale green eyes that could be stern but would not be now. You Know Who was sipping a Damn the Weather—curaçao, orange juice, vermouth, and dry gin on cracked ice—and feeling, from the moment that Daphne first smiled at him, that he was auditioning for a role the nature of which was being concealed from him. "I think my father's book would make a wretched movie," Daphne now confessed. "I only wrote to you about it because I wanted to meet you. Your face in your films reminded me of a boy I once loved. We were both maybe six and we were on a beach somewhere, I don't remember where, my father took me to lots of beaches even though he didn't much like swimming. But one day suddenly there was this little boy beside me and side by side we sat building a vast sand castle that didn't seem to need water to hold together, the sand was so obedient. The little boy had brown curls. The castle had seven outer walls with seven outer gates. With all its towers and turrets, it rose up higher than our heads and in each tower we stuck a twig with a gum-wrapper flag. Our hands were touching as we dug together for the sake of speed and depth. His eyes peered out at the world and at me but kept running back. He couldn't stop them from doing that.

76

Neither can you, can you?" You Know Who parried the question with a confession of his own: "My films are terrible. No producers in their right mind would back a project in which I had a major part. There is no way I could get your father's book made into a movie, even if I gave a damn about filming it, which I don't. But there was something about your letter that made me think you were confusing me with your father, which in my experience can be a symptom of passion in a woman. So naturally I wanted to meet you as well." "Please do not compare yourself with my father. He was caring when he was not absent, which was often, and his book—he said I gave him the title for it, but I don't remember that—is like the jottings of an aquarium fish that swims back and forth but finds no way in or out. But you are my beautiful boy on the beach who vanished and found his way into the movies." "And out again," added You Know Who, who decided then to shut up and let Daphne have her boy.

HECTOR TURNED THIRTY-FIVE IN 1935 on the day he disembarked from
the tramp steamer that had taken him from Bombay across the
Indian Ocean and through the Gulf of Aden to the port town of
Obek, which lay in French Somaliland just south of the straits that
linked the gulf to the Red Sea. Here Hector met, in a café, a fellow-
born Frenchman named Henri de Montfried whose Arabic name
was Abd el Hai and who sailed the Red Sea in a boutre named Ibn
el Bahar, *Son of the Sea,* which de Montfried took himself to be. Profit
and adventure were his two avowed aims, but underlying them both
was his love of the solitude of sailing by the winds. He boasted to
Hector of having published a book devoted to his earlier voyages —
titled *Pearls, Arms, and Hashish* in its English-language release. De
Montfried exulted in the life of a Red Sea "smuggler," as he liked to
call himself, and the author's photo for his book showed him
standing upon the boom of his boutre, furled sail beneath his feet,
scanning the horizon for his bearings, bare-chested and lean, a
kaffiyah wrapped about his angular head with its hatcheted features
and those moustaches tapering to finely upturned points. Hector
described his own book to de Montfried, who rubbed at his chin as
he took in Hector's narrative approach of letting little episodes run
around after each other. "I gather then," de Montfried said at last,
"that you have never embarked on a voyage — the wind at your back
and clouds darkening the horizon — upon the outcome of which not
merely your worldly fortune but your very life depends. Now there
is a narrative worthy of the telling. My poor friend, you should sail
with me for a time — but as an apprentice-mate, not as a tourist."
Hector thought it over as de Montfried sipped his richly sugared
espresso and helped himself to one of Hector's gold-tipped Egyptian
cigarettes. The offer played neatly into Hector's fear that perhaps

his book (as yet untitled, Daphne being as yet unborn) lacked a central ripping yarn. That evening, in his room on the second floor of a cheap dirty hotel in a back alley of Obek which he had chosen to escape his ubiquitous life of luxury, Hector felt himself losing his nerve: "There are times when we pursue temptations which we know full well to be unworthy, for the sole and passionate purpose of being pulled out of realms in which we have dwelled far too long. If this man de Montfried leads a life that in any way approaches the grandeur of his talk, then I shall be happy to serve among his piratical crew. And loathe though I am to admit it, perhaps the braggart can teach me a thing or two about writing." As for de Montfried, that night he spoke to the chief mate of his crew of four, Abdi, a Somali man of indeterminate age who wore a white fez and was the surest of guides in the Red Sea waters: "Abdi, this new man Hector, make it seem for him that he is one of us." Abdi pondered to himself the word "seem," which he understood to indicate an illusion clung to as truth. He made up his mind to teach Hector the rudiments of sailing and to leave the rest to Hector himself. In this, Abdi tacitly demonstrated why he had no taste for authorship, while de Montfried, who viewed Hector as a potential secondary character to layer into his next book of adventures, couldn't wait to observe the transformation of a mild and moneyed traveler-at-whim into a browned Red Sea smuggler with a silver-hilted dagger.

DE MONTFRIED HAD A WIDE READERSHIP in the 1930s, and with good reason. He was a knockabout, a stylish raconteur, a tough guy and a romantic loner who fit in poorly with his fellow Europeans and was altogether the "other" among Africans and Arabs. He traded in pearls and rifles and drugs but drew the line at slaves, for whom brisk markets remained in existence that were fostered by the greed of Europeans, Africans, and Arabs alike. This residual streak of honor made de Montfried a source of frustration for both the customs agents of Britain and France and the insiders of the Red Sea smuggling trade. De Montfried, in his books, was pitiless in portraying their mutual corruption and decadence, but he harbored no personal hate for them — his sense of contempt was too great to tolerate their lingering presence in his soul once he returned to sea. The taste for de Montfried's books ended with the start of the Second World War, during and after which his adventures no longer seemed as adventurous as once they had. Now and then he is rediscovered by some reader and then forgotten again. But when Hector met him, he was just beginning his ascent as an author and just past his prime as a smuggler. De Montfried drank more than he used to, though he still cared little for the hashish and opium that traded so abundantly in the region and made the fortune not only of the dealers but also of the colonial and local officials who collected biweekly baksheesh for noticing nothing amiss. If de Montfried had an erotic or an emotional life, he kept it to himself. When, now and then, Hector began to moon over Elise, de Montfried would say, "Whether for a woman or another cause, a man will find a way to be a fool," and shake his head, appearing to laugh at both Hector and himself. During the time of their friendship, de Montfried devoted himself principally to pearl fishing, darting his agile boutre into hidden narrow bays and joining his Somali divers in the underwater hunt for the pearl oysters known as *ʃadafʃ*. Hector tried diving but found, after several attempts, that years of heavy smoking had not contributed to the strength or capacity of his lungs, and so rather than give up smoking he brooded over his degeneration and remained on shore slicing open the oysters retrieved by the others and removing any pearls he found. Hector learned to tell the difference between a desirable "live" pearl and a "dead" one that had lost its luster from remaining too long in the innards of a deceased oyster. He became productive at this work and enjoyed cooking up the oysters as well, which made him better liked among the Somali crew. De Montfried caught the spirit of the thing and managed to wrangle some butter and garlic and tomatoes and herbs with which to flavor a cauldron of bouillabaisse that Hector prepared on shore on the eve of their departure from a particularly rich array of oyster beds in the Gulf of Trajura. The Somalis obtained pitas from a household a mere four miles roundtrip by foot. While they were gone, de Montfried produced a bottle of Bordeaux. "When they see Europeans drink," he explained as he swigged and passed the bottle to Hector, "it is to their eyes what seeing a man fuck a goat is to ours. And so their presence can ruin the taste of even a fine wine. Drink up, Hector, it will allow you to enjoy your own cooking all the more." They combined to finish off the bottle in a matter of moments and had a fun and lovely time out there on the harbor shore smelling the stewing oysters and pretending not to be drunk when the Somalis returned with the pitas, like the Somalis couldn't tell from the shit-faced smile bleeding across de Montfried's face as he fell asleep on the beach bloated after dinner.

Hector stayed awake and listened as Abdi spoke of his desire to obtain his own boutre someday. While de Montfried slept and the rest of the crew prepared for the dawn casting off, Hector opened his money belt and gave Abdi what was to Hector half the amount of one of his monthly coupons from one of the dozens of bonds which Muir had bequeathed him. The amount was sufficient for Abdi to procure his own vessel at the end of the voyage. In this way, Hector felt himself to be convincing Abdi that he, Hector, was not as drunk as the snoring de Montfried. Abdi concluded that the foolish Hector was far drunker than de Montfried had ever been. Abdi kept his windfall a secret, as he feared that his fellow crewmen would otherwise cluster about Hector eliciting his good will and thereby spoil the pleasure his captain de Montfried—who would soon be calculating bonuses for them all—took in this strange man's always uneasy presence.

Abdi, shortly after purchasing his own boutre.

HECTOR PARTED COMPANY with de Montfried in Alexandria, where de Montfried had gone to spend some of his pearling profits on black-market antiquities, while Hector was content to frequent the city's museums by day and bordellos by night. The two men had a last dinner together. De Montfried selected the dining room of the Hotel Metropole as the site to bid farewell to their life as fellow salty dogs. Again, as on the beach, they drank fine Bordeaux. De Montfried became a bit maudlin, though his sentiment was lessened by his utter inability to draw, from Hector's months of service on the *Son of the Sea,* so much as a single scene for his next book. As best as de Montfried could figure it, Hector lived a kind of life that always stopped just short — he could have risked drowning by pearl diving but instead he just found something else to do. Hector's wealth didn't help; in truth, de Montfried pitied his foppish friend as a spoiled victim of the excessive kindness of an infatuated London tippler. The two men drank and laughed, now and then they hugged, they devoured lamb couscous with chutneys. Hector basked in the affection shown him that evening by the Red Sea smuggler, though he also rankled, in secret, at the none too subtle jibes by which de Montfried made it known that he regarded Hector as a mere pretender in the world of manly adventure.

"IT WAS, AS ALWAYS, A TIME of unrest in the Arabian peninsula," Hector wrote much later that night, ashing with particular intensity into the cobalt-blue ashtray engraved with the name of the Hotel Metropole of Alexandria. "My rash friend de Montfried—whose political sympathies were with the Arab rebels who struggled, as de Montfried did, to shake off their European fetters—had agreed to deliver a shipment of rifles and explosives to a hidden inlet on the southern Arabian coast. Sympathies aside, the potential profit to de Montfried was immense, as were the potential dangers to Abdi and myself and the rest of the crew. There was, indeed—for all the loyalty the Somalis felt toward Abd el Hai, as de Montfried insisted on being addressed by them—a definite prospect of mutiny or, worse still, betrayal of Abd el Hai and his accomplice, yours truly, to the British authorities in Aden. De Montfried was drunk, metaphori-cally for once, with the publishing prospects that such a smuggling adventure could afford him, and we saw him smiling to himself all through the surreptitious loading of the deadly contraband into the hull of the *Son of the Sea* in the dead of night. At dawn, we set sail from Obek, the wind at our backs and storm clouds on the horizon, engaged in a voyage upon the outcome of which not merely our worldly fortunes but our very lives depended. De Montfried stood at the tiller and grinned and helped himself to my Egyptian cigarettes as always. We sailed east/northeast, skirting the harbor of Aden in which the authorities lurked, en route to a destination known only to de Montfried—such was his precaution against betrayal. Little did he reckon with the plan hatched by one of his Somali crew to seize the boutre by force and to sell its cargo to rebels of his own choosing, for there was no lack of buyers for arms along the Arabian Coast. De Montfried had a way of sleeping lightly at the tiller, and this time it

85

cost him dearly. The mutinous Somali slipped behind him and, with his left hand, placed the fine edge of a dagger across de Montfried's throat, while, with his right, he pointed a Wembley automatic—a favorite handgun of the British colonial police—at the rest of us. 'We sail the course I set!' the Somali commanded, while de Montfried gaped but did not dare to move a hairsbreadth. Abdi, the chief of the crew, remained calm, and his two mates seemed to look to Abdi, rather than to de Montfried or the mutineer, for an indication of what to do. When Abdi turned his eyes to me, they did likewise. I nodded to them and smiled, as if to instruct them to set the new course demanded. In the moment of calm gained by my ruse of acquiescence, I lunged head forward like a bayonet into de Montfried's belly, causing both our captain and his assailant to topple backwards, the latter badly banging his head against the mizzenmast and dropping his Wembley but not his dagger which he flailed in vain against the empty air where de Montfried's throat had rested a second before. But de Montfried had scrambled away and now sat panting in terror at my feet, while I seized the fallen Wembley and kept it trained at the mutineer's head. Abdi fetched a rope and bound him to the mizzenmast. I passed out cigarettes to the loyal crew and together we smoked while de Montfried, who had roused himself somewhat, resumed his stance at the tiller. His usual taste for my cigarettes was in abeyance—perhaps the brush with death had led him to appreciate the joy of breathing simple air through his throat. Abdi gazed at me for a time, then asked, 'You have not taken for yourself an Arabic name as has Abd el Hai. Why is that?' He spoke to me not as Somali to European, but as man to man. Carefully, so as to give no offense, I explained to Abdi that my name Hector de Saint-Aureole was the sole keepsake I had of my youth and so it was precious to me. Abdi smiled, then said, 'So you are not a man who cares for seeming-to-be, as does Abd el Hai, who owes you not only his future arms profits but his very life. He is fortunate to have you as a friend.' Two days later, de Montfried made his coastal rendezvous with his rebels. Let all hell break loose, so long as we are paid in British pounds! Such was the mood of captain and crew alike. De Montfried counted out a lavish cut for me, all of which I passed on to the crew, with the lion's share to Abdi. All of them asked that the mutineer be set free, as he was a countryman with a family. De Montfried longed to make trouble for him with the harbor police, but I patted de Montfried on the back and said, 'My friend, when they see a European make trouble in a world in which the law is white, it is to their eyes what seeing a man fuck a goat is to ours.' De Montfried burst out into a guffaw and relented. Shortly thereafter, I resolved—while wagering to my profit on the cutthroat cockfights in the alleys of Alexandria—that there were adventures enough on dry land for me to renounce the life of a Red Sea smuggler, even as I hoped for the best for my friend de Montfried, who had come to seem to me strangely out of his element at sea."

IN BARCELONA, during the last weeks of peace before the outbreak of the civil war which he fled as did all travelers without purpose, Hector met a gaunt woman with a mouth like a slash and eyes that searched the horizon. She was one of the locals who competed for coins to serve as guides for travelers wishing to tour the Gothic and Ribera districts in which remains of first-century Roman walls intertwined with labyrinthine stone streets in which shops and cafes and churches alike were hidden. All this the woman conveyed in a guttural but fluent English, as she took Hector for a Canadian. After they viewed the Cathedral of Santa Maria del Mar, with its interior arches reaching toward heaven like a vast gray glove in which the hand was invisible, Hector suggested they rest for a few minutes on the edge of the gray stone stairs that extended down into the hectic city square in which fruits and vegetables were sold from packs on donkey backs and the cafés plied large clear glasses of dry rum and tiny white cups of bitter coffee and an old street musician whose guitar was nearly beaten through sang in the *cante jondo* style that wept. So that the woman, whose age could have been fifty or eighty, so taut were her features, would feel at her ease, Hector paid her the agreed fee for their tour and added a large gratuity, which sums she thrust at once into her purse. Hector offered her a Turkish cigarette and they both smoked in the salty haze of a Mediterranean midday. The woman, having observed a period of silence, inquired if the gentleman was wealthy. Hector nodded yes, finding the question both impertinent and forgivable, for after all, the poor could never conceal their poverty, while the rich could masquerade as petit bourgeoisie. Let the truth out! The woman then inquired if Hector was married. Hector lifted his left hand to her, turning it about to display the lack of a wedding ring or of any jewelry whatsoever, not so much as a watch, for Hector seldom needed to know what time it was. He proffered the woman this emphatic assertion of his bachelorhood, though she—the wearer of a wedding band—should have seen for herself. But perhaps she mistrusted married men with removable rings and was about to make an offer to betroth to him her poor but beautiful and saintly daughter. Why are you not married, the woman inquired, and now Hector felt annoyed at her taking his invitation to rest and smoke as an invitation to disclose his life. But then who else but this crone cared to hear his reasons? Two women only I have loved, he told her, and both of them failed to love me in return. You are a woman, you tell me why. She asked for another cigarette and he gave it and lit it. You are rich but clumsy at love, she then advised, you must leave it to the woman to find and measure you like the timber she needs to build her home to her own desires. Hector felt ferocity arise. Old woman, tell me of the man whom *you* found and measured and cut to your standards. Her eyes lowered, her lips spat. He was faithless to me and died by the hand of the Catalan husband he wronged thirty years ago. Do you grieve him? Hector asked. Let me tell you how I grieve him. The man who murdered him became my husband after his adulterous slut of a spouse died by the hand of a Catalan wife.

HECTOR SPENT THE SECOND WORLD WAR years in Buenos Aires. He did not propose to volunteer himself for military or other service. It would have been a torture to adapt to any sort of schedule after nearly two decades of the utmost freedom. And he was afraid of the war, of Hitler especially; he wanted to be far away from it and Argentina seemed that. As a sop to his conscience he arranged— through Barclay the solicitor in London—to forfeit his claim to £10,000 worth of British government bonds, a minor holding in his inheritance portfolio. This passive donation to the cause enabled Hector to listen to the speeches of Churchill on the BBC without shame. Within a few weeks of his arrival in the city, he struck up a friendship with three local men whom he met at a chic boulevard café. One was a cattleman with extensive land holdings to the south, one a composer whose work was being compared to that of Villa-Lobos and Milhaud, and one a marvelously funny fool of a waiter. This waiter could magically impersonate the voices of Hitler and Churchill—his pièce de résistance was a screaming match which he carried on both in belligerent mock-German and sententious mock-English with expository asides in Spanish and French; he had the gift of making no sense in any language, the waiter would say of himself. One night, seated separately at the bar, the cattleman, the composer, and Hector found themselves laughing in unison at the waiter's antics. Having revealed their shared contempt for the politics of the world, the three men went on to confide to each other the adventures of their lives over further drinks. It became an all but nightly ritual. Hector, the cattleman, and the composer each possessed personal fortunes. The waiter, who was poor, came over the course of several months to rely upon the generous tips of the three men to fund a lifestyle far beyond his accustomed means—one that included French wines, Cuban cigars, a used Fiat coupe, and women who had always loved the waiter and loved him not the less now that he bestowed upon them jewelry and perfume. Hector, the cattleman, and the composer were always served the strongest drinks—the barman took care of that for a cut of their gratuities. One evening, after several rounds, and with the waiter already off for the night, the cattleman nodded pointedly to the composer who then proceeded to explain to Hector that there was a private gentlemen's club in the city, to which both the composer and the cattleman belonged, where a form of dueling, technically illegal, was enacted now and then, as the occasion arose, and that tonight was such an occasion. Would Hector like to attend as their special guest? They felt they knew him well enough by now to rely upon his discretion. Hector accepted immediately; it seemed to him that he was being invited to bypass the limitations of a foreign tourist and to witness firsthand the degraded customs of the wealthy underbelly of Buenos Aires without risk to himself. It might all make for a tidbit or two for his book. The composer and the cattleman—insisting that hiring a cab would only create a trail for busybodies—led the way on foot through dark side streets to a forgotten brick edifice at the outskirts of the city. After passing down two flights of unlit stairs, they reached the entrance to a columned cellar once used for the storage of wine and produce. The cellar was now thickly carpeted, with tapestried walls and rows of leather armchairs along three of its sides to accommodate an audience of roughly twenty. An elderly gentleman of evident means—dressed in black tails, with an emerald tiepin, and on his fingers three rings encrusted with gems and intricate symbols signifying Hector knew not what—spoke

91

briefly with Hector's two friends and then, turning to Hector, eyed him as if to say, I will remember you for good or ill, then beckoned him to proceed. The composer, the cattleman, and Hector sat side by side. The lights were dimmed at ten P.M. precisely, and two hooded attendants commenced the proceedings by wheeling forth a large rack to which a gagged and blindfolded man was bound. This man, Hector soon discerned, was the waiter. He turned to the composer and the cattleman who briefly gestured as if to say it was a surprise to them as well, but what was one to do? One of the hooded attendants then called forth the aggrieved challenger who had demanded the duel. This proved to be a member of the club whose son had been befriended and then dishonored by the waiter—a pretender to wealth and style who was in fact cosmopolite mulatto Jewish homosexual scum. The nature of the dishonor to the son was not specified. The aggrieved challenger explained that he had arranged for the waiter, on leaving his shift this very evening, to be kidnapped and brought here by force for a duel that offered better than the waiter deserved—the impersonal justice of fate. A crack marksman, the club pistol champion, whose dispassion as to the outcome of the duel had been attested to by personal oath, would, at a distance of twenty paces, fire six shots at the one-inch target rim painted closely around the contours of the waiter's head, which had been firmly affixed in place so that no panicked movements by the waiter could affect the outcome. If the marksman were accurate six times in succession, the waiter would have the sound of shots ringing in his head for the rest of his life, a fit punishment in itself, and one that would dissuade him from ever mentioning the incident. The marksman was sworn to take all six shots, regardless of the number of inaccuracies along the way.

92

Theoretically, the waiter could be shot in the head six times, although that had never occurred; the record for a challenged party was three, and the marksman employed on that occasion had never again been asked by the club to perform this service, which the club provided to its long-time members so as to assure that they would never be forced to endure the bumbling delays of even properly bribed Buenos Aires policemen. Hector wondered if there was anything he could do for his friend the waiter, whose body, should he perish, would surely disappear, with nary a word ever spoken of the duel thereafter. Could he save the waiter if he tried? On the contrary, he would be killed by angry club members, among whom would be the composer and the cattleman, whose eyes were now fixed upon the seething face of the mute waiter. Hector had yearned to explore the underworld and here he was already its minion. Perhaps the waiter would live and they would all laugh at this over drinks tomorrow night, slap the waiter on the back and chide him for keeping such secrets as to the breadth of his erotic conquests. The first shot rang through the cellar and out from the waiter's gagged mouth came a vomited scream. A hole in the target rim showed clearly as the rack was backlit for that very purpose. Six accurate shots would create a corona of light around the waiter's head, and Hector recalled the days when he too had been a barman in The Midshipman's Watch waiting on old fools like his benefactor Muir. Had Hector not become a benefactor to the waiter? And yet he would sit and do nothing. Shot two. A silence. A shudder throughout the room. Hector sank into his chair and saw a second hole of light. The waiter, after some seconds, groaned. Then shot three—the marksman was free to time and pace his shots as he liked, but it seemed to Hector that the groan had been taken by the marksman as a kind of affront and so the third shot was quick just to shock the waiter back into silence. It missed both the target rim and the waiter's head, which must have been a rare sort of miss in such duels, for there were coughs and snorts from some of the audience members. The sound that now dominated the cellar room was the hard breathing of the marksman. The waiter was so weakened by this point that only the ropes that bound him head to foot kept him from dropping to the floor. Shot four found the painted rim and created a topmost star for the corona. Hector was beginning once more to enjoy the experience. The marksman truly had no animus toward the waiter. Two more accurate shots, or two more shots wide, and the waiter would live and Hector would help him to get away from Buenos Aires and its crazy rich men who killed those whom their sons chose to love. Shot five drew blood from the waiter's left temple and the waiter choked on his gag as sobbing took hold of his body. Shot six went straight to the waiter's heart. The body flinched and shook as if it would wring free of the ropes and then it slackened so completely that the ropes seemed fooled and nearly lost their hold. There was knowing laughter in the room, not only from the ones who had snorted and coughed just moments before, but from all the club members, including the cattleman and the composer. The loquacious introduction of the duel, its sequence of shots, all had been intended, Hector now understood, to intensify the torture of the victim as he went to his preordained death. Hector left in the company of the cattleman and the composer, wondering how the three of them could ever speak to each other again, given their complicity in the murder of their friend. But strangely it went easily. They all agreed that a return to their café would be in order, as drinks would calm their nerves and drinks at that locale would pay suitable homage to their late friend. It seemed to Hector insanity—a precipitous return to the scene of the crime—and yet, as the highest magistrates were members of the very private club in which the duel occurred, there would be no investigations. The waiter was no more, it was only that. But as they approached the café, Hector made an excuse, he said he felt ill. He thought to himself let them think of me what they like. He said he was weak and homeward bound and would see them soon, very soon at the café. Profuse thanks for the experience of which he would never speak as—this went unsaid—he didn't want to die like the waiter. Hector didn't so much as dare to write of it in his own book—only these three lines were entered that night as he smoked the American Lucky Strikes that were widely sold in Buenos Aires: "The war is everywhere. It was folly to hide. Leave Buenos Aires tomorrow and never linger anywhere again."

HECTOR SAT BEFORE A PINT of stout in Maeve's Pub, which was set in an old thatched farmhouse and named after the goddess and queen whose cairn atop Knocknarea across the bay rose like a nipple from a breast of grazing sheep. An ancient fiddler in a stained coat, patched pants, holey socks, and unraveled shoes sat beside a turf fire and sawed out a mournful aire that enveloped the fiddler more deeply than even the smoke that the chimney flue forbore to draw away on this winter night with its thick shawl of snow and rain without. The publican was approaching seventy, Hector fifty. The publican's daughter, who when necessary wiped the tables and dried the pint glasses—at present Hector and the fiddler were the only patrons, the former playing and the latter paying for his pints—was perhaps thirty. The publican gazed upon her and smiled as fathers will when daughters have consented to remain beside them longer than custom bids. This publican had florid cheeks, bushy white sideburns, and flattened buttery hair combed across his spotted skull-skin that stretched from ear to ear like sausage rind. The daughter had long, well-brushed hair, brown or gold according to her nearness to light. Her face was covered with brown-gold freckles that varied in size from grains of sand to kernels of June corn, and beneath them all was skin the color of the milk from the local farms served each morning in a little blue jug as Hector breakfasted in his room at the Great Southern Hotel in Sligo town. Hector wanted to speak to the daughter, whose eyes were the soft blue of the earliest clear skies after sunset and whose smiles were to herself. Hector imagined she was thinking of escaping her father and his pub, but what sort of escape was making her smile? Raising such questions with her was impossible with the publican watching. So instead, Hector sipped at his stout and smoked Player's cigarettes, offering one to the publican, who sat awaiting little but the one A.M. closing time. He nodded assent to the offer and Hector struck a match to serve them both and they shared a yellowed ashtray in the figure of a mermaid. Hector now asked — recalling his days in The Midshipman's Watch and the unabashed drunkenness of its patrons when time and circumstance seemed to them to call for it, as it did for Hector now — how many pints of stout could the publican's patrons drink, on average? The left eye of the father now lifted, due to his having observed Hector dawdle a half-hour on his first pint. But the English — so he took Hector to be — enjoyed asking stupid questions as they drank, and perhaps the answering of it would lead to the Englishman's further purchases of pints to test whatever consumption limits the publican, now shrewd, might choose to set. "Seven would be what the best of my customers could abide." He gestured toward the fiddler. "Old Emmett there will be at five if he downs his foam." Hector promptly ordered six more pints to be set before him, which the daughter did with a smile, though whether she was pleased with Hector's daring or refraining from laughter at his foolishness, no man in the pub that night could say. For Hector, there was no turning back. Having drawn the daughter near to him, briefly, the only way he could, he now drank down the six pints the way he'd seen it done in earnest in The Midshipman's Watch — head back, down the throat in two or three swift swallows, catch the gasping breath, wipe the besotted chin, belch out the suds, repeat. The daughter still would not smile to other than herself and Hector became a fool on the chance he could change that. The clock behind the bar — set among spigoted upside-down bottles of whiskey and the decanter-figure of an Irish soldier in red breeches and green waistcoat with gold brocade — struck one and the fiddler ceased playing and the turf fire beside him seemed to ebb with the silence. The daughter came close once more to remove the empty glasses that stood between Hector and her father. So quietly did she remove them that the wind and rain outside roared all the louder. Hector rose, donned his fine tweed coat with fur collar, and asked the permission of the father to request the company of the daughter on a walk to the Golden Strand this coming day at noon, an hour of innocence. The fiddler had vanished, leaving Hector alone with the publican and daughter in stark after-closing electric light. The father turned to her. His daughter now eyed Hector as she would a dog come to the back door begging. She was wearing a gray sweater and a long gray skirt and laced black boots over woolen stockings. But for her freckles, her ears and lips and neck and wrists and fingers were unadorned. "My daughter will speak for herself," said the publican. The daughter then said to Hector: "Sleep off your stout and be here at noon precisely or not at all. If I am to have a walk with a strange man, he will be a prompt man to convince me to take my leisure with him." Hector nodded assent, keeping his weight back on his heels to prevent swaying. He then bid them both good night and, falling forward, stumbled out the door, slamming it behind him. As he sloshed to the cab he had hired to wait for him, he paused to piss a yellow streak in a newly fallen heap of snow. The cabby, as he opened the passenger door, silently cursed the rich drunk for not so much as standing his driver a round at the bar. Within the pub that served also as house and home, the father observed, as he switched off the lights and poured ashes over the glowing remains of the peat, that with his payment for drinks and an outsized tip, this man who had given his name as

Hector de Saint-Aureole, of all names a strange one for an Englishman, had paid their way for weeks. "He is unbeholden," said the daughter named Una, who mopped at the counter where the foams from Hector's stouts had overspilled. "There is a beginning in that. No more."

UNA AND HECTOR TOOK THEIR WALK and Hector, insofar as he could discern his effect upon persons, felt himself to be functioning at his best with her. He asked her questions of a gentle and expansive order to which she could reply as briefly and vaguely or lengthily and precisely as she might wish. He did not flirt with her but simply kept to her walking pace and allowed her to look at and listen to him and to form whatever opinions she might form—he was past believing that he could talk a woman into love with him. What he could convey was that he was attentive and kind, moneyed and lonely, and wanted a woman who looked and moved and smiled and spoke like Una. Just how he knew this so surely was not clear to him, nor did he wish it to be, indeed he wished his thoughts would cease and leave him free to focus completely on this woman, on this walk, his one chance with her. He was getting old, he had few passions left in him, he could feel them dying off one after the other over the years, the passions for eating and drinking, for seeing and walking, for sex without talking. He wanted to curl up beside a woman who smelled a bit like milk and who would grant him peace. And in return let her ask for whatever she might wish, he would have no more wishes of his own left to make. Hector asked Una if she had grown up here where they walked, if she enjoyed her work in the pub, if the weather was often so gray with scudding clouds and cold as it was today. She had, she did, and it was. Una had no intention of indulging him by spilling the story of her life, which in her view a man ought slowly to earn knowledge of, chapter by chapter. Furthermore, if this Hector had no idea quite what he wanted to know, she did and would. She asked of him his age, the precise means of his fortune, of Muir and The Midshipman's Watch, of his years of travels, and of the source of his silly name which he had surely invented—but no, Hector explained, Saint-Aureole was the family name and he had retained it as a dare and dared to live by it as the one sacred light by which all souls seek their truth. I hope, Hector added, that by saying this I have not offended your religious beliefs. My religious beliefs, Una said, are not such as are capable of offense. But tell me what have you come to treasure in all your years with your sacred searching light? I have come to see, Hector said—making it up on the spot as we do in conversation when we are invited to give sense to a lifetime of stumbles and missed ways and losses—that treasures are not mine to have, not even when they are placed into my hands. Not even, Una asked, when they are placed very softly and tenderly? An erotic shiver ran through Hector that nearly knocked him into the roadside ditch. He kept his face straight so as not to show any of this and kept walking at her pace, answering all her questions with the best explanations he had, keeping consciously from her only that he was at work on a book that took him into the night now and then.

UNA KEPT HER EYE ON THE OLDER MAN, watching his face far more than she took in his words. She had never much believed the explanations of men as to why they did or did not. She regarded men as in the nature of fiddles that could be plucked at by a knowing hand so as to determine their range and tonal quality. The choice of tune mattered little so long as the notes were true, as they were with this older man whose soul she strummed. He believed himself as he spoke to her, this much she knew, and he was pleased to please her and trusted both in her goodwill and her practical bent as allies in winning her over. She would be taken in by his earnest adoration and lured all the more by the money. And how was she to see herself as seen by him? As a younger woman with a lilt to her and a focus in her gaze that lent to her beauty a power sufficient to clean out his life of its unwanted things, the hot-water bottles and whiskey flagons of lonely male middle age. He spoke of his travels in the manner of someone who has eaten overmuch and badly, a state she had never known and ever detested. Still, this Hector had kept himself reasonably fit, a sack of manfat falling down upon but not yet over his belt. His hair was thinning all over his head, his temples included, but she could find him a cap, of all things, in Ireland. His face was that of a dog that had once been a lovely puppy but now has stiffened, faded eyes with which it still pleads with intent grace, only rarely barking and on those rare occasions is sorry afterward to the point of distress. From the way Hector spoke, Una saw that he had evaded being weighted down by his wealth—a trunk of clothes followed him like a donkey on his travels, a safety deposit box here and there, but no permanent residence, no shelves of books, no desk and globe, no plates and table and chair and hearth of warmth that he himself tended. Small wonder he had come to the pub of a cold winter's night, small wonder he had taken her for a fire.

UNA LED HECTOR TO THE NEARBY Golden Strand, which was not golden but rather a bracelet of heaped gray rocks offered to a gray onrushing ocean that would at last, long after all of this, grind them to fine sand. In the midst of the begloomed afternoon, Una took off her green tweed coat and then her boots and wool stockings. She was left in a brown sweater vest, a white blouse, and a full black skirt. The skirt she hitched up well over her knees by means of buttons and holes that she had sewn specially for such usage. Una then waded into the water, and Hector took in her bodily sensations as they were conveyed to him by the strength of his fascination for her, and found himself shivering on the strand and wishing he had, in addition to his coat, worn a cap. She played in the waves, washing her legs and her face with cupped palms. She made no sign to Hector to join her and, other than waving to him once in a friendly fashion, seemed neither to sense nor avoid his gaze, which was steady. Without wishing in the least to wade, he rolled up his pant legs. Then he walked into the receding waves that urged him on to her side. Should he try to kiss her? Una took his hand and gave his palm a little scratch with her ring finger. They walked further in slowly together. Hector's pant legs came loose as they always did when he tried to roll them up tightly. Una said she would have to sew him some buttons specially. He brought his face close to kiss her and never in his life had he seen a woman so unchanged by the nearness of his face in its quest for a kiss. She neither shut her eyes nor shook a warning nor considered him as anything unlike the wind or the ocean about her. He kissed and she kissed back and the kissing went on until there was no clear sequential order. It was the best kissing for Hector since the dreams of youth with the succubi. It was the kissing in which the very taste of the saliva is good. During the kissing, Hector became many other men in many other times, all of whom were kissing women at the ocean's edge. He never heard from those men again. They vanished, and he was still standing kissing Una, who noticed Hector's daze and kissed him with all of herself.

ONE OF THE READERS OF *When to Go into the Water* was an unaffiliated Breton neo-Druid who insisted, on the basis of his visionary readings of the astral traces still lingering on the Golden Strand in the year 2000 from the encounter of Una and Hector fifty years prior, that Hector had been overcome and inhabited by a Druid shaman of ancient times, who seized on the chance to control Hector's fortune and from it to make financial restitution to at least some of the people of this Celtic land for all that had befallen them since the lies of Patrick and the slaughters of Cromwell. According to this theory, a possessed Hector gave out sums of cash to whom and in such amounts as Una bade him. As for Una, who was neither Druid nor Christian nor other, she felt clear unto herself as to which of her neighbors needed help and how much, now that it was affordable. Her father, for instance, was given a sufficient sum to shut down Maeve's Pub and retire in peace and even to hire a servant to tend to him as the withering of extreme age set in. For Una would be gone, off with Hector up and down the world. A woman down the road, mother of four, husband killed in the Irish Civil War, was given funds to purchase the small farm she rented. In Sligo town, there was an old laundress with hair so white it seemed bleached, who had suffered a herniated disc and could no longer bend and lift as she needed. A sum was given to her so that she could settle back. An amount so large it was termed a "donation" was given to a hospital in Bundoran. All the while, as Una saw it, she was helping Hector to save money by having him move from the posh Great Southern Hotel to her own bed in a small back room of the pub, which her father continued to operate despite Hector's bequest, as it wouldn't do to let the extant stock of whiskies and ales and stouts go to waste, nor would it do to have the distributors think they were to leave the place high and dry. That Hector and his daughter consorted together while he worked the pub out front he knew and didn't care for but couldn't cry about, having done his own share of cavorting under the nose of Una's late mother, whom Una was out to revenge was the way the publican saw it, but musha she'd found a means to her vengeance that paid well. The father wasn't himself a religious man but it made one think. Back in Una's room, with its plaster walls painted the blue of a gray sea, they spent as much time talking as consorting on what was a small bed in a stuffy room with a single window, only a tiny center pane of which could be opened. Sometimes, lying scrunched together, Hector listened eyes shut to the radio at low volume—an Irish station of news and operas and Catholic sermons, with the news and sermons read, to his ear, as beautifully as the operas were sung—while Una, who had no interest in writing a book and no knowledge that the man beside her was doing so, read mysteries and modern romances and now and then a pamphlet on the subject of bicycle maintenance. Una was a fearsome cyclist and preferred to ride alone rather than lag back for Hector. Nor would she allow him to buy her a new bicycle even though he asked to, the one she had suited her well enough and she had the time and will to maintain it. The few writings composed by Hector during these first months of domestic acquaintance were set down through a haze of late-night cigarettes. Una saw smoking as a waste of money and an embrace of filth and preferred he do it in their room only while she slept. Faint-breathed she was in her rest, and Hector adored to look upon her and then to ash in a Tennent's Lager ashtray and then to turn back to the work which had until now emerged from deepest solitude. So was it envisioned and insisted upon by the unaffiliated Breton neo-Druid.

"UNA," HECTOR WROTE, infatuated by her role as the latest and, to his mind, best character in his book, "has confided to me a dream that has occupied her since her childhood, and that I am able easily to fulfill. In the dream, Una as a little girl was bestowed a special power by the Queen of the Fairies—the power to choose which of her memories to banish and which to keep. The ones she banished would be banished forever, along with the pain that inhabited them. But the ones she kept would serve as little holy wells, revealing more of themselves each time she gazed upon them in earnest. Alas, the Queen brought the dream to an end before Una could make her decisions. Since that dream, Una has longed to own a camera and to teach herself to photograph, for in that way she believes she can bring the power bestowed by the dream to her real life. She desires no instruction other than the printed operating manual that comes with any camera—more than that would be an interference with the power that must be hers alone. Of course, Una has never been able to afford a camera and film and darkroom utensils and chemicals. All this I have granted to her—a Leica camera and an unlimited account at the photography shop in Sligo town. My reward, alas, is that I see her far less, for she is off pedaling on her bicycle and snapping pictures the whole day long. When, at last, she returns it is only to work through the night developing and printing her visions which for the first several days were blurs and blots but have since metamorphosed into cows with heads that fill the sky, and spiky thistles that stand proud as medaled generals, and a moon crashing headlong into a trough of water, and a husband and wife standing outside the door of their cottage waving hello at the lens and wondering at why Una should ever wish to have their picture. Una has turned her bedroom, or dare I now say our bedroom, into a darkroom out of which I am kept for long hours. As a result, I have taken to drinking with the old publican after hours. He has discovered, to his self-satisfaction, that so long as he weaves into his stories of a life spent in idleness and vice some account of the young Una and what pleased and displeased her, I will not only listen but also pay the bar tab for the both of us and then some. One story he told remains with me especially. When Una was nine, her mother died of pneumonia, and Una said to her father as she held her dead mother's hand that her mother's spirit had passed into her and henceforth he'd best behave, for the two of them together would tolerate no longer his drinking and whoring of the past. So frightened was the father by this that he dared not disobey his daughter from that day to this. In truth, I do enjoy this father who has lived a life that has pleased him well and who seems ready to die without fuss. His heart, I feel, has been put to rest as concerns my intentions toward his daughter. For I explained to him that I had asked Una to marry me and was, to my sorrow, refused on the grounds that had Una wished to be married she would have been so by now. She was perfectly willing to stay by my side for as long as she could foresee, and as for the child she wished us to conceive, it would upon its arrival be in her care always, and mine as well if I could keep up with the two of them. 'Yes,' the publican chuckled at me, 'that'd be she. And I ask you, what more could a fellow wish than his freedom by her side?' It seemed futile to try to explain to him that, having never won the hand of a woman, I felt it the obverse of freedom to be refused a legal right of place cozied up against her under the blankets of life's winters. Still, she makes me breakfast—toast, jam, two soft-boiled eggs, stewed tomatoes, no rashers or puddings or bangers, as they are dear in cost and steeped in the stench of the slaughter of animals—every morning and serves it to me on a tray in bed before she pedals off. And she kisses me goodbye before she goes, first carefully wiping the toast crumbs away from my lips."

IT WAS UNA WHO WAS WANTING TO SEE the world that Hector felt he had already seen. So Hector now traveled for the pleasure of being with Una. After so many years of walking alone in strange cities, it gave Hector a dog's satisfaction to walk beside her and be guided by her steps. She would tug at his sleeve to make him pay attention, always with the hope that this faint thoughtful man would catch fire. What Hector liked best were their late weary evenings in hotel beds falling asleep together, Una's hair and skin and smell beside him. For many years, they agreed that having a child would happen naturally. But it didn't, and as Una began to approach forty and Hector sixty, it seemed to them both that it would never be. By telegram received in Istanbul in 1958, they learned of the death of Una's father, whose funeral Una had Hector pay for but would not herself attend, saying to Hector: "I saw my father through the last decades of his life. He can see himself through death." Una was taking photographs as they traveled through the fjords of Norway, the steppes of the Ukraine, the quays of Odessa, the Hindu Kush so far as Peshawar, the Himalayas from Baluchistan to Kashmir. Una had a fondness for mountains, having been raised in sight of Ben Bulben and Knocknarea. She tried to catch the mountains in her photos and couldn't—the pictures she made were no better than postcards, she could see that for herself and it ate at her. One night, it was in Djakarta, Hector asked if she'd thought perhaps she should go to a younger man to get her baby before it was too late. She hushed him by lulling him into sex. Una knew the baby would arrive this night. She held her body still at the end to catch it from him at last.

Hector and Una at a masquerade party,
Lisbon, circa 1956.

IT WAS UNA'S DESIRE TO PHOTOGRAPH manatees, alligators, egrets, and other swamp creatures in their natural habitat, so they embarked on a liner from Tangiers to Miami. Una was nauseous both from her pregnancy and the surging and swaying of the liner. Hector was so veteran a traveler that his stomach regarded the rollings of the sea as familiar and soothing. He spent his time loving Una and holding her hand at nearly every opportunity, including while he slept, as Una informed him. She understood it as umbilical, the father wishing to join with the baby in the intimacy of connection with the mother. Nonetheless, she insisted on her own daily solitary time, which she spent snapping pictures of the people on the ship when they weren't watching. She snapped them as they ate their chowder and drank their gin martinis with green olives and chatted over cards and cigars and brandies and oyster crackers. She snapped the chefs and pursers and officers and swabs and cleaning crews. She took to snapping the doings of the passengers in their staterooms if their curtains weren't closed and the light was right. This new development in her aesthetics Una kept to herself. Hector, she reflected, had a prurient mind and would have objected to her artistic tactics on the grounds of propriety and potential legal exposure. Una, whose mind was sated with prurience from her young years serving drinks to drunks, wanted only images that sang life—and would have them. Whatever she could see she would take.

THE DAY AFTER THEY DISEMBARKED from the liner, they hired a Seminole guide to give them an automotive tour of the Everglades, during which Hector viewed stretches of grasses like masses of raised swords, in which dwelled stalk-legged scythe-beaked birds yellow as tallow, pink as taffeta, gray but spotted bloodily with red. The guide, Osceola, described the war between the Seminoles and the American forces led by Andrew Jackson in a tone that reminded Una of the elder folk in Ireland recounting the Famine. Osceola had Seminole friends who wrestled alligators at a tourist stop, should Una and Hector wish to see. For Una, the mixing of wrestlers and gators would have spoiled the photos she wanted to take of just gators. For Hector, the prospect of witnessing men paid to thrust their heads for show between gator jaws triggered a phobic response. Hector had, from time to time, wondered if he had previously been alive and if he would be reborn. He had been surprised to find just how comfortable he felt with the prospect of being reborn as an animal. The life of a marmot or a trout or a sparrow seemed far more to his taste than the life of a human child struggling to adapt to the absurdities of human expectations. But now, as they drove, Hector saw alligators on the roadsides and creek beds and culverts, and as he considered their rippling armor and muscled legs and claws and fangs and eyes like they were seeing him dead already, Hector decided that humans had achieved something meaningful after all, and he patted Una's ripening belly. They declined Osceola's invitation and asked him to take them back to their hotel and they assured him that, based on his fine safe driving today, he could serve as Una's well-paid guide over the weeks to come when she would be touring the swamps and coastal shores in the hopes of catching nature at its doings. Patience, Una had learned, was of the essence, for solitude was rare and nothing was always found anywhere.

Florida fruit stand and patrons, photo by Una Cargadon, 1963.

THERE WAS A SAVVY HORSEPLAYER at a track near Homosassa Springs where Hector spent a great many of his days while Una went off to snap her pictures. The horseplayer's name was Nelin Ginginger, and he wore red-striped seersucker suits and red silk socks and a straw skimmer with an alligator-skin band into which was plunged a flamingo feather. Nelin's face was like a flattened grapefruit and when he drank his fruit drinks from a straw—Nelin would not touch liquor himself but seemed to relish drunkenness around him—it seemed to Hector that the straw was sipping out of Nelin to fill the glass in Nelin's hand. It was through Nelin that Hector learned a method of handicapping that worked as well as any other, according to Nelin. Instead of focusing on past performance times on fast or muddy tracks or recent wins by the jockey—all the standard racing-form info printed off for the suckers—take the time to walk over to the paddock and check out the horses as the grooms give them their pre-race warm-up strolls. Right at the start you can eliminate from betting consideration any horse with sweat-frothy flanks or groins—that means they're anxious and leaking energy badly. From the rest of the horses you pick the one with the best ass. What's the best ass for a horse? The one that seems most defiant is the one you bet to win. If it's a close call, bet the almost-best ass to show just to cover expenses. Pure and simple. Trust your gut for picking the asses you like on horses the same way you pick the asses you like on women, not that I picked my woman for her ass, Nelin explained. Just what he did pick her for Nelin never told Hector, who assumed that, like most men, Nelin not so much picked but took the woman who could most stand him, for wasn't that Una to him even though he adored her? The woman who lived with Nelin in a one-bedroom apartment that she kept neat, and who sometimes accompanied him to the track with a sack of devilled eggs and potato chips for the two of them, was named Oval Embofsed. She was from Kentucky and liked to play slow airs on the dulcimer with her one good hand and her one prosthetic hand during the evening hours so as to soothe Nelin, who was always worn out from the track. It was work pacing back and forth from the paddock to the betting window and then to the grandstand chair to watch asses in binoculars coming round the home stretch. Oval's face was like an unpeeled potato scrubbed so clean that the remaining skin is as pale as a window shade in the moonlight on a night a child is born to a mother who already has too many. She and Nelin were both somewhere in their forties, younger than Hector, yet to Hector they seemed older as they'd been a shack-up couple for years without producing children, while he and Una were unmarried but expecting. Hector, who had money to lose, started betting the ass system and had some good days and smoked and drank at the high-roller's bar at the track. Nelin, who claimed he had a job somewhere but showed up at the track every day Hector was there, which was every day, died in his grandstand chair on a July afternoon during the half hour between the fourth and fifth races. Nelin had just placed a bet for that fifth race, then sat down on the chair he had saved for himself by leaving upon it a cushion embroidered with his initials and a picture of a racehorse by Oval and, boom, heart. Turned out he hit the fifth-race winner that paid long odds. Hector, who had dropped by to compare ass picks with Nelin, found his friend dead. They phoned Oval from the track infirmary. She arrived some twenty minutes later in sneakers and a sweatsuit that hid her ass and with wet hair like she'd just been washing it. She looked down at her dead man in his seersucker suit, squeezing both her good hand and her prosthetic hand tightly. Hector whispered in her ear about the winning ticket that had been in Nelin's shirt pocket, and he now gave it to her good hand, then left the room as Oval cracked open from sobbing. Hector went back out to the grandstand—the tenth and final race of the day was about to start, not enough time left to check out the asses in Nelin's honor. Instead, Hector lit a cigarette and wrote on the back page of his track program: "A man who depended upon luck to live found that luck could not protect him from dying. And I stood helplessly by his slumped body, friend and fellow fool. Is there a lucky life? Am I living it? Perhaps many people would say that I am. But when I saw Oval sobbing, I realized that the truest good fortune is not to outlive the one you love." That night, in their hotel room, Una cleaned her camera lenses, brushing her graying hair back behind her ears as she worked—and all the while, Hector marveled, she carried new life in her belly. He came up beside her and kissed her neck and smelled her sweet milky skin and wiped away tiny bits of swamp flora that had settled behind her ears as she went about ducking and hiding and snapping in the wilds. Hector tried that night to write more about Nelin's death and about love but instead fell asleep, and in his dreams he was trying to die before Una did, and Una was holding their baby and screaming "Coward!" at him. He awoke in a sweat, touched Una's sleeping belly, apologized to the newborn-to-come for his heedlessness in seeking to depart before his time. He fell asleep close to the skin of the womb and dreamed now of the succubi of his youth saying goodbye, flesh is but flesh, the passage is done, time to train the new crew, don't bother to rush at death, it's rushing at you.

OSCEOLA WAS A KNOWING and flexible guide who, for lavish tips Una told Hector nothing about, assisted her in pursuing the line of photographs for which she had developed a taste on the cruise ship to Miami. There were out-of-the-way motels frequented by white tourists and managed by Osceola's Seminole friends who were happy to be paid to fail to observe a noticeably swelling white woman bundled up in a black coat and a black stocking cap approaching the windows of the tiny cabins that came complete with kitchenettes. The spring of the shutter of her Leica was merely an insect buzz, Osceola assured her, especially if she kept well hidden. But Una would wander close to windows now and then, for, without knowing the whole bleeding history of photography, she knew no one had ever snapped them like this before.

ONE OF THE POTENTIAL READERS OF *When to Go into the Water* was Edwina, a craftsperson of the year 2059 who was adept at fashioning jewelry boxes out of fine old editions of books that few people cared to handle any longer, since they had access to millions of stories in goggle-shaped screen and audio format controlled by the programming tastes of the begoggled. So say you wanted to experience *The English Patient* by that Canadian guy, you could access any of the four film adaptations and, if you wished, select new wardrobes and accents and races for the actors to better suit your own experience of deathless love. You could even—if you had enough poscreds to delete for the best unit made—program visions of yourself and whoever else you wanted to play the scenes of erotic frenzy and wasting away. So Edwina, when she found nicely made old books, reconstituted them to take advantage of their silks and vellums and linens. She was lucky enough to find ten copies of *When to Go into the Water* in a box in the basement of an old building her Texarkana boyfriend had purchased and was now rehabbing. He was happy to make her a gift of stuff he didn't give a damn about, and she was delighted with the grain of the marbling of the handmade pages. After cutting out the textual centers so that the margins could frame an elegant space for jewelry storage, Edwina sliced the potentially wasted text-paper into strips she then dipped in green ink and thatched into a tropical-hut look for the covers of the ten book-boxes, leaving only the word *Water* from the original embossed title still showing under a layer of aquamarine lacquer applied over the exposed vellum.

HECTOR, UNA, AND THEIR DAUGHTER DAPHNE remained in the United States but had no settled home. They traveled in Chryslers Hector bought new every year as every year they drove well over 100,000 miles. Una preferred to photograph on the fly, going off by herself to the strangest places at the oddest hours and then ready to move on, while Hector had come to realize that, for him, travel would never stop. When Daphne was five they enrolled her in a pricey nonreligious but altogether staid and well-appointed boarding school for young girls in Kansas, as that was a central state they could criss-cross through during their perpetual driving. In this way, Daphne was able to see her parents one weekend per month September to May and then all through the summer while essentially living her own life which, even at age five, Daphne greatly preferred, as she liked what she liked and nothing else. At age five, Daphne exulted in the oversized leather-cushioned library armchairs with their view of the prairie grasses as refracted through stained-glass window portraits of the philanthropic founders of the school, the name of which was Wishiwass Academy, which Daphne took to pronouncing as "I Wish I Was A Can of Me," which made her a hit among her fellow kindergarten boarders, few of whom saw their parents as often as Daphne saw hers. Una and Hector always brought Daphne dolls and costume jewelry and pralines and home-baked pies from the best roadside cafés, and sometimes, sometimes not, Una let Daphne see her film negatives through a magnifying glass in the shape of a spool that Daphne could clutch with her fingers. Then would come alive stark silhouettes that mirrored, for Daphne, her black-and-white dreams, for Daphne could not dream in color. Once, at night, as Una was tucking her in—they were on the road, it was summer,

121

Hector was off in a corner writing and on such occasions he preferred that Una pretend that she did not notice him — Daphne asked her mother if her dreams were like that too. Una told her that the nighttime was the time for the dimming of color, it was good for the soul to sink into its protective shadow to rest and, while resting, to see the essential forms of our lives without their gaudy distracting color displays. And that is what I do with my camera, Una explained, it's my way of dreaming in black-and-white film even while I'm awake. To illustrate the effect of this for her daughter, Una completed a series of photos in very low light of Daphne serene and lovely just after she'd fallen asleep, and for the rest of her life Daphne looked forward to going to bed and passing into that joy. Once when Una and Hector were driving together, just the two of them, Una at the wheel as she was more and more — for more and more Hector preferred to stare out at everything and let it pass through him, relinquish it, rather than drive — he asked her, without anger, just to understand, why she snapped everything in the world except him? Una answered, my dear darling old heart you are my camera, I carry you with me and I never let you go, but I never think to photograph my camera, and I would far rather see you freshly daily.

THE WEDDING OF You Know Who and Daphne de Saint-Aureole took place in December 1999 in the remote Alaskan lair that You Know Who would now be sharing with his bride. The hand-printed invitations sent out to a select three dozen or so persons included a statement from the couple "that this be an Old and not a New Millenium wedding, for we are not fooling ourselves entering our forties." It was, to Una's way of thinking, far too dour a stance to strike in a wedding invite, and her daughter's stance it would have been, for her son-in-law had neither the wit nor the heart to bridle together love and regret just so. Una gazed out a wall made entirely of windows at the ferocious froth and fanged cliffs of the Alaskan coastline. The house in which her daughter would now live out her years, assuming the best, was filled with paintings and rugs and soft places to recline. The hired staff were serving the best Russian vodka in the frostiest shot glasses that stuck delightfully to Una's fingers each time she went to the bar for a new one. There was a Unitarian minister from Juneau who performed a ceremony written by the bride and groom in which Daphne promised to "abide by the side of a man who needs to learn to sit down without wondering what the chair is thinking" and You Know Who swore to "stay by the side of the little girl who once dreamed of her castle and has now, with the help of her unworthy prince, found it, I hope." The paparazzi would have loved to crash the ceremony, as photos of You Know Who were always of interest to a public hungry for his mix of supposed sex and seeming eccentricity, which would make the public wonder all the more whether his new wife was sexy and crazy too? The truth was that Daphne could be both, but certainly not all the time, and in photos she tended to look annoyed by the camera. Given the geographical isolation of the house and Daphne's

123

determination not to wind up on the tabloid front pages, the only photographer present at the wedding was Una, whose incessant absences to go off snapping during Daphne's childhood had made cameras, if not photos, quite obtrusive to the bride. Daphne wanted an album of her wedding to look over during the long Alaskan nights as the fire blazed and You Know Who rubbed her feet and they would try to have a child or adopt and wouldn't the child want to see pictures of Mom and Dad on their day, so why not hire at no cost her own loopy mother? And if Una wanted to put together, out of the raw imagery of a joyous occasion, an arty little exhibition portraying what Una saw as the tragedy of the marriage of her vibrant daughter to a Hollywood stiff, well then Daphne and You Know Who would attend the opening—the publicity would be good for his film career, the best directors would see that he was starting to open up to the world again. Daphne posed with her groom for Una who was drunk and laughing as she took the shot on her knees from under a table. Later Una tried lying on the floor looking nearly passed out and then snapping the asses and crotches of the guests who were stepping over and ignoring her. But if they spilled drinks or slopped food, she sat bolt up and snapped their faces. The only shot she took special care with was of the strawberry wedding cake with marzipan icing, beside which rested a copy of *When to Go into the Water* and Daphne's handwritten note: "This is the book that brought us together." That would have pleased the old fool, Una knew, and she went off to sample the buffet of Alaska king salmon with truffles, field greens, and aoli and thought of Hector who had once said to her that he enjoyed seeing her enjoy food more than he enjoyed food itself. He was, she thought, an earnest giver of compliments, and she missed him, eating alone in a corner tonight.

EARLY IN 1967, THE YEAR OF HIS DEATH though he never knew that, Hector arranged for the publication of *When to Go into the Water* through a commercial printer in Texarkana whose usual work was on tourist brochures and instruction pamphlets for home-appliance assemblage. It was a wonder—of which the printer spoke to the end of his days—when Hector first walked into his office with a walrus-skin briefcase full of cash and utterly deluxe specifications for a book that was to bear the imprint "privately issued *hors de commerce*" (the printer would be paid in abundance but condemned to anonymity) and to feature a Holland-backed binding with vellum covers and two green-silk ties to be undone to enter the interior realm of pages of Van Gelder handmade paper bearing Hector's text in Caxton Antique typeface, with a colored lithograph frontispiece—specially commissioned by Hector—of Una and Daphne as sad winged naiads hovering over fearsome crashing waves in which the author of the book seemed to be drowning. The print run was limited to two-hundred copies, fifty of which Hector sent to prospective reviewers, the rest to varied and widespread acquaintances including Barclay the London solicitor, Henri de Montfried, and the Catalan wife. These latter he inscribed effusively, but Hector heard back from none of them while he lived, and if they wrote thereafter, it is a certainty that Una would have tossed their letters, not being one to pry into correspondence not addressed to her. As for the review copies, dispatched to publications great and small, only one bore fruit—Hector's book was cited as a "solid account of getting one's life's feet wet" in *Riparian Rights Monthly*, the publisher of which was a client of the Texarkana printer and had been sent a copy by mistake. The Texarkana printer remained annoyed at receiving no credit for his quality custom work, though the paycheck for the job had enabled him to buy forty retirement acres just outside of town. Money aside, Hector had tried to explain and had at last insisted to the printer that mystery, beauty, and scarcity were the essential keys to the ultimate survival of his book through the years—hence the lack of a detailed provenance, the sumptuousness of the design, and the limited run—from which a backup supply of ten copies would be stored by the printer subject to later shipping should Hector so direct. In private, Hector fumed over the eight errata slips that had been so costly to prepare and insert into the volumes on the eve of their debut. He could not rightly blame the printer, for Hector had left the page proofs to Una to correct, reasoning that a fresh reader of his work would have a better eye for errors, and reasoning also that Una would surely be reading it anyway so why not usefully now? Una neither found it compelling reading nor could spell (how would Hector have known, as they had never been apart since first they met, and hence no letter of Una's had ever reached Hector as they did her "farther bak settin in the wett boggies") and so she pronounced the book "brilliant" after a week of carrying about the page proofs in a semblance of absorption, nor did she deem that pronouncement a lie as for all she knew it was indeed brilliant, having been written in the quiet of night by her dear Hector. The worst of the errors that found their way into the book had Hector praising "a check of hose" rather than "a cheek of rose," though the reader who read Hector's book in the bathtub while smoking Chesterfields took that as an artfully naughty reference to fishnet undergarments, which were in truth more interesting to Hector than rosy facial cheeks, all of which demonstrates the revelatory instability of all texts and the justness of Una being regarded as a de facto collaborator, though the book's title page bore Hector's name alone. For all this and that, Hector was at heart enchanted with his slim bound effusion, as authors are.

IT WAS OCTOBER AND THE BOOK was out in the sense of demonstrably physically present and they had just visited Daphne at Wishiwass Academy and were heading for the Dakota Badlands which nobody visited that time of year they figured, too cold. But the roadside cafés would still be open serving Folger's coffee and hashbrowns pan-fried in butter and onions and homemade cinnamon rolls bursting with raisins and slathered in icing. Una was most interested in snapping the people as they ate in the cafés but she was eager to capture the razory rock formations as well, for from the brochures she'd seen—the Texarkana printer had graciously provided them with plenty, and not only for the Dakotas but for everywhere in the continental U.S., the trunk of their Chrysler was full of them—the Black Hills were the earth gone mad and Una felt she could work with that, such had her confidence as an artist grown since her early days of being daunted by mountains. Hector was driving that day, a rarity, and felt himself grow queasy and then a pain throbbed in his chest and grew in intensity minute by minute until, in Lead, South Dakota, Hector pulled over, had Una take the wheel, and whispered to her to find a hospital. What passed for such in the town was a two-story turn-of-the-century wooden house with its resident doctor on vacation as the tourist trade always dropped away in October. The nurse on duty was Agnes, a Norwegian in her sixties who knew enough to sit Hector in a wheelchair and to listen to his heart with a stethoscope and to say that it was beating too fast and making him sweat and go pale. Agnes gave him aspirin and a sedative and by eight that evening he was in deep sleep. Round about midnight, as Una sat in a chair beside Hector's bed, Agnes came in to check his pulse and blood pressure and to listen again to his heart. She lifted his eyelids to study his pupils and Hector did not awaken. She let them drop, and then the white face of Agnes took on the stillness and symmetry of a mask. "Some nurses have second sight," Agnes then said to Una. "I have known for a long time that I have it, but I have never told anyone of my gift. Tonight I must make an exception, because I can see that you are someone who lives by the clear light of simple truth. Your husband is going to die." Una smiled at the nurse and replied: "He is indeed going to die, but not here and now, no." For Una was immune to convictions of second sight, many a patron of Maeve's Pub having claimed the same as she served them their pints. Una then suggested that they leave Hector to sleep and have themselves a cup of coffee together at the nurse's station where Una had noticed that Agnes had a pot brewing. As they drank, Una showed Agnes her camera and persuaded the nurse to consent to being photographed as she made her rounds from room to room in the small hospital, the other patients being a young girl with the measles, a farmer with a leg mauled by a thresher, and a lunatic. All were asleep and Agnes consented as well to Una's snapping them in the dim light with Una's assurance that they would be unrecognizable. It was the first time that anyone had shown interest in Agnes and her hospital for themselves, Agnes felt, and she saw in Una not only a widow but a sister. The next morning Hector awoke and paid the bill. Agnes tried to persuade him to stay but Hector replied that the surest way to die was to remain in a hospital bed of one's own free will. Fifteen years later, in 1982, when Una had her first one-woman show of photographs at the Vertiginous Gallery in the North Beach district of San Francisco, it was her sequence of hospital photos—titled "Night of Second Sight"—that won the highest praise and fetched the highest prices, not that Una needed the money, for Hector's ample estate had been split between Daphne and herself. As for Daphne, when she did bother to phone her mother, she never failed to mention that critical praise be damned she found Una's photographs exploitative and creepy. Whereas Daphne had just drifted through her twenties and thirties as she pleased, it seemed to Una, who could not help but admit to herself that she resembled her father in this. Una dwelled for not the last time upon Hector's passing, which occurred in November 1967. Someone had slapped him on the back, thinking wrongly that they recognized him, and his heart gave out that instant. It was in a Chicago bar and he had been drinking, waiting for Una to finish with her snapping for the day. When the slap hit, Hector looked up at himself in the mirror behind the bar and then was no longer there.

DAPHNE WAS PLAYING ON THE BEACH on a chilly lake in the North Woods that her daddy had visited way before he met her mom. Back then her daddy had heard some story from a French guy that he tried to retell to Daphne and her mom one night, but neither one of them got it and Daphne wasn't even sure her daddy really got it given the winding way he told it. Daphne was seven and she got a lot more than her daddy thought she did. She got that, at Wishiwass, she had to write her name as "Daphne de Saint-Aureole," which sounded to her like the name of a crazy bird in a crazy cage, and all because her daddy wanted her to have his name while Mom got to have her own name, Una Cargadon, which was way better. Daphne knew that her daddy, who was sitting on a beach towel in a bathrobe because the sky was cloudy and he wouldn't swim with her unless the sun broke through, was lonely because Mom was away so much with her camera. That was what they had in common on this day, the two of them. But would he come swimming with her so that they could both have fun? Oh no. Daphne stared at him and she let him see that she knew how afraid and tired he was, even though he was sitting there reading a book and pretending the book was making him smarter and better. Her daddy had told her once that he was writing a book and that she was in it. She had told him back that she didn't want to be in his book or anyone else's and that made him laugh like he knew she would outgrow being so silly—the same laugh as the teachers at Wishiwass had. Now can we run into the lake together Daddy? He shook his head no and kept reading and she asked when and he said maybe if the sun got hotter and she said he should write a book about when to go in the water. Then she went back to digging in the sand, wetting and slapping together a castle with a secret back

131

stairway by which the princess who lived there could escape. Just then, without her having noticed, a boy with brown curls and eyes that peered out at the world and at her but kept running back sat down beside Daphne and offered to help.

Daphne in her snorkeling gear, photo by Una Cargadon, 1967.

Photo by Sarah Sutin

THE AUTHOR

Lawrence Sutin is the author of *A Postcard Memoir* (2000) and of two biographies—*Divine Invasions: A Life of Philip K. Dick* (1989) and *Do What Thou Wilt: A Life of Aleister Crowley* (2000)—as well as of a historical work, *All Is Change: The Two-Thousand-Year Journey of Buddhism to the West* (2006). He is also the editor–author of *Jack and Rochelle: A Holocaust Story of Love and Resistance* (1995). He lives in Minneapolis and teaches in the MFA and MALS programs of Hamline University and the low-residency MFA program at Vermont College.